Emperor of the North

Emperor of the North

of the

a novel by

Christopher Knopf

BearManor Media

2016

Emperor of the North
© 2016 Christopher Knopf

For information, address:

BearManor Media
P. O. Box 71426
Albany, GA 31708

bearmanormedia.com

Typesetting and layout by John Teehan

Published in the USA by BearManor Media

ISBN—1-59393-899-3
978-1-59393-899-4

DEDICATION

*To Jack London, Jim Tully, Josiah Flynt, and all the rest
lesser-known, long forgotten, who lived this.*

Hobo and Railroad Slang As Used In *Emperor Of The North*

HOBO SLANG (*In order of appearance*)

ALKI STIFF: Perpetual drunk
STEW BUM: A booze fighting bum
JUNGLE CAT: Can take anything anyone throws in his path
YEGG: Roving criminal of trampdom
TRAMP ROYAL: Primordial nobleman of the road
FAKIR: Con man
GAY CAT: Tenderfoot
MUSHER: Itinerant repairman
PEG: Leg amputee
BO: Hobo

RAILROAD SLANG (*In order of appearance*)

COALY: Fireman
HOGGER: Engineer
SWITCHMAN: Manipulates switches
YARDMAN: Essentially a non-commissioned officer of
    the rail yard
YARDLET: Apprentice yardman
DISPATCHER: Controls movement of trains in and out of
    yard

YARD CLERK: Maintains records of train movements
YARDMAN'S HELPER: Assistant to Yardmen
GROUND HOG: Engineer
OP: Operates telegraph
GREASEBALL: Engineer
MUDHOP: Yard clerk
DINGER : Conductor
ASH EATER: Locomotive fireman
GAFFER: Section boss

Prologue

WESTERN NEBRASKA, OCTOBER, 1931.

No breeze blew on the prairie. Not a cloud was in the sky. Insects droned lazily along the rails. Ahead, the plains stretched like a checkerboard, squares of late summer corn, yellow, and brown. The wistful cry of a locomotive. A rift of smoke on the horizon trailed the sound.

In a stand of cottonwood trees a hundred feet from the tracks and a turnout leading to a water tower on a siding, stood a jungle camp where three hoboes boiled coffee in a tomato can. Ears cocked to the approaching sound, they listened, ages varied but of one breed, and low order at that, common vagrants, encrusted with gutter filth and untrimmed beards, Alki-stiffs and Stew Bums, with little self-respect, but on their way wherever destiny might lead. Suddenly, a rumbling was heard, like the rolling echo of thunder. Some quail, startled, flew from the cornfield, and the ground vibrated, the train moving into view, slowing. As the hoboes watched, a trainman, the brakeman, lowered from the engine, hurried forward to a switch, bent the switch bar, stood back as the train eased off the main, onto the siding.

In the jungle camp, the hoboes grinned at each other, exploded into activity. The fire was kicked out. Belongings were thrown into scattered unrolled bindles, ragged clothes and shoes, empty and smoke-blackened cans, some dog meat partly wrapped in brown paper, some pieces of broken glass, a can of Sterno. The train, not ten cars in length, lumbered toward them, onto the siding, its heavy engine trimmed in orange.

On the side of the engine, Coaly, the Black fireman, waited the approach of the tower as the engine slowed, steam spiting from cylinder cocks. A figure, backlit in silhouette against the light, stood on the step at the end of the tender, holding to the grab iron, leaned out over the roadway.

The three hoboes had wrapped and tied off their bindles. Hoisting them to shoulders, they turned, moving eagerly, broke from the cottonwoods out onto the side of the roadbed, twenty yards up track from the train, drew back to a man, frozen by what they saw. On the nose of the engine, sliding toward them with a hiss of expiring steam, was a number, '19'. A chill ran through them as they pulled back into the trees, their gaze turning to the figure riding out the slowing train as he clutched the tender's grab iron.

With a great squeal, the train lurched to a halt. The figure's boots, immense, rope soled with metal scuff guards at the toes, lowered to the ground, moved up track. He was the train's head man, called Shack. Not any Shack. *The* Shack. A long familiar dreaded sight, he was known and feared and for reason. Eyes cold and piercing, his face, except for a scar and moustache, was smooth and hard. His size was enormous, as was his strength. He was in his forties, with the force and will to put fear into any hobo. His train, this train, '19', was his domain. Nobody rode without a ticket and, if tried, he collected, one way or another. He moved, never stopping, searching couplings and bumpers and rods, across the opposite side the train, then back again.

On the tower catwalk the Hogger, the train's engineer, lowered the downspout. Atop the engine, the Coaly had already opened the water intake hatch, grabbed the downspout, guided it to and into the opening.

On the ground at the end of the train at the turnout, the brakeman stood by the switch. He was a physical, frenetic little man, a Georgian, called Cracker, honed and trained by the Shack, as a dog trained for war.

As the hoboes watched, fearful and marveling, the Shack moved up train offering not so much as a glance toward them in the trees, no more than one would regard fermenting yeast. He reached the point of the engine, continued past it, up track. Behind him, the engine puffed like a tired horse. Whirls of smoke coughed from its stack. Ahead of the Shack, there was nothing in sight except the rails bisecting the prairie. The Shack drew to a stop, twenty yards up track from the engine.

In the woods, a fourth 'bo—the slang they called a Jungle Cat hobo—who'd earned his spurs against trains, flattened himself against a tree, held his breath, not daring to breathe, a man about thirty-five, tough and seasoned by years on the road. His bindle, attached to a stick, hung down by his feet.

The Shack didn't move. If he'd seen the hobo, he gave no indication of it. He stood there, mid-track, exposed in the open, staring up track, as motionless as the hobo, no more than forty feet from him. After an interminable thirty seconds, he turned.

In the trees, the Jungle Cat let out a shuddering breath of relief as the Shack moved back down track toward his train, swung aboard, disappearing from view. Atop the engine, the Coaly capped off the intake, closed the hatch, lowered to the engine's catwalk, entered the cab, opened the fire door, took up a shovel, and began loading the firebox with coal from the tender as the Hogger came off the tower, and disappeared inside the cab.

The Jungle Cat drew a tentative finger across his mouth. Had the Shack seen him? Or was it the three quavering bums at the edge of the woods? He looked back at the train. Eight cars, he counted. As he watched, the train began backing off the siding, returning to the main 'til its engine cleared the turnout. The Cracker bent the switch bar, closing the switch to the siding, the engine resting for a moment, snorting, when it began to ease forward, up the main. The Cracker, waiting out the passing cars, reboarded at the caboose. The engine, a reluctant beast of burden, threw itself against its load, slowly picked up speed.

The Jungle Cat took full measure of the now passing freight. To board or not? The engine passed, and the tender. Then a reefer, gondola, and box car. As the three lesser hoboes watched, incredulous, from their sanctuary, the Jungle Cat went for it, broke from the trees, ran forward with the train, caught the grab iron on the box car, swung himself quickly onto wooden bumpers. A glance toward the engine, then back at the caboose. He'd made it. No sign he'd been detected. He settled back, reached inside his shirt pocket, pulled out the stump of a smoke, when there was the impact of feet against metal steps! It was a sound to put dread in the stoutest tramp.

His response immediate, reflexive, he started to move off the opposite side of the train. Not fast enough. The vicious swing of a darkened lantern was brought crashing down, the globe splintering on the hobo's head. He fell, down between the bumpers, tried, with one desperate effort to keep from going to the tracks, but the wheels grabbed the cuffs of his pants, sucked him under with a rending shriek.

As the three hoboes stared in horror, the Shack, holding a grab iron with one hand, swung out over the racing roadway, the smashed lantern in his other, looked back at the hobo going under the train, a lifeless mannequin buffeted rudely about with each passing car.

The Shack held, viewing his handiwork, looked toward the Cracker staring after the hobo from the end steps of the caboose, nothing startling in the sight, all in a day's work.

1

THE '19' POUNDED EASTWARD. The wrench and tear of couplings, iron on iron, brake shoes throwing off sparks, the chatter and screech of wheels, the lurch of undercarriages, straining at rods, the blur of the roadbed and pounding drivers, the buck and heave and sway of the cars, lost, then seen again in smoke and a shower of red-hot cinders trailing back from the engine's stack; Plunging down track, smoke laid flat over trailing cars, '19' roared through the farm belt of Western Nebraska.

Twenty miles down track, an empty stock car stood on a siding off the main. A golden place, corn stalks high, a golden hour, shattered by the '19', plunging, slowing, dragging its compliment of cars to a halt past the turnout to the siding, whirls of smoke curling from its stack. Nothing else was in sight. A breathless day, not a tree, not a house. But the cornfield was concealment for the hobo.

Clutching a live chicken in his fist, he pushed through stalks to the edge of the field, peered down track at the train. He was a large man, heavily muscled, of indeterminate age. From his appearance, one would say he was phlegmatic, slothful, withal without passion, and quite soulless. In fact, his mind was crude and strong, and controlled a brutal, life-scarred body that had long since earned him the moniker, A-No. l. His hair, topped by a soiled hat, fell in straggly red masses over his ears and neck. A newspaper stuffed into his hip pocket, his coat was torn, showing gape-like tears under the arm pits. He stared down track at the train as though sizing up a snorting bull.

At the end of the siding stood an empty stock car. The Cracker swung lazily off the caboose, onto the ground. Throwing the switch bar, he signaled forward to the engine. In the cab, the Coaly shoveled coal into the fire box as the Hogger reversed the train across the turn-out off the main, onto the siding to pick up the empty, the engine's drivers squealing, iron on iron as the air cut in.

The hobo pulled back into the corn, moved between stalks across furrows. A coffee fire smoldered between two rows. A tin of simmering liquid stood over it. A blanket was laid out on the ground, a few meager possessions atop it: a pair of unmatched shoes, some ears of corn, a straight razor, a broken piece of mirror, a heavy shirt, and a "ticket," a 3 x 5 piece of pine wood, grooved down the center, used for riding the rails.

Pouring the liquid from the tin, the hobo tossed it on the blanket, his bindle, pocketed the straight razor, slipped the "ticket" into his rear hip pocket, bent to gather the rest in his blanket. He stopped. Before him stood a youth. Dressed in what he had begged or stolen, he was sixteen, medium height and blond, wily, volatile, treacherous, his untamed energy and insolence a howl to the gods. His name, fanciful and self-anointed, was Cigaret, and his eyes feasted on the chicken in the older tramp's fist.

A-No. 1 brought his head up slowly, every movement of muscle, from the heave of his shoulders to the tightening of his mouth a warning. When suddenly they were on him, small dim forms, snarling and strange. They were Road Kids, five of them, six. Twelve to sixteen years old, Cigaret their leader. They were the cubs of trampdom, herded together like wolves, and like wolves capable of stripping and gutting the strongest man. They came at A-No. 1 from all sides, squealing and screeching like demons, flinging themselves upon him with every ounce of strength of their wiry bodies, quick dark forms with gleaming eyes, teeth bared and flashing.

Into A-No. 1's back went Cigaret's knee, around the neck from behind passed his right hand, the bone from Cigaret's wrist pressing against the older tramp's juggler as others clung to his arms and legs, trying to wrest away the chicken. A-No. 1 never let go. Even as teeth sunk into his neck, he lashed out, whirled, infuriated, cursing, sent them spinning, plunged into the corn, his bindle abandoned, but not the chicken.

Maddened by the vision of the tramp laid bare, Cigaret left the confusion of the others, headed after A-No. 1 alone, broke from the corn field onto the tracks. The train, he saw, had crawled off the siding, back onto the main. Cigaret ran ahead of it, back and forth across the tracks, searching the edges of the cornfield, left side, right, no sign of A-No. 1, the train now slowly closing, forcing Cigaret to commit to one side of the track. The engine passed. Then the tender. Then two freight cars.

On the opposite side of the train, A-No. 1, chicken in hand, sprinted from the corn, ran forward with the train, caught the grab iron one handed on the third car, a reefer, swung onto the bumpers at the end of the car. A glance toward the engine, then back at the caboose, A-No. 1 ran a hand across his neck, annoyed by the blood. But he still owned the chicken. He settled back, when there was the impact of feet against metal steps.

His response immediate, A-No. 1 was off the opposite side of the train, barely in time to avoid the vicious swing of a four pound hammer as the Shack pounded aboard.

A-No. 1 did not look back. The Shack's footsteps on gravel told he was pursued. Reaching the head of the reefer, the tramp boarded, intending to cross over, onto the original side of the train. But the Cracker was racing forward from the rear of the train to intercept, brake iron in hand. Only a split second to decide, A-No. 1 climbed, one-handed, chicken in the other, up the iron rungs to the roof of the reefer, into swirling, low lying choking smoke from the engine's stack.

Atop the box car, A-No. 1 scrambled to his feet, the train, gathering speed, offering little foundation as he ran back along the heaving deck. Reaching the end of the roof, he grabbed the shaft of the brake wheel, started to swing down the end ladder but the Cracker, anticipating the move, sprung onto the bumpers below, reached for A-No. 1's foot, grabbed it coming down.

A-No. 1 lashed out, drove his foot into the brakeman's shoulder, missing the sweep of the Cracker's brake iron as it struck the brake shaft, A-No. 1 dropping off the end of the car out of sight.

Clutching his hammer, the Shack came off the roof of the reefer, onto the following car. Eyes cold and piercing, he searched couplings and decks, looked back through swirls of blinding smoke toward the engine, then to the end of the train again, holding to his jog no matter the sway beneath him, legs spread wide, taking the buck and pitch of the deck like a practiced mariner.

The caboose was the next to last car. Coming off it, onto the roof of the empty stock car just picked up from the siding, it was attached to the caboose.

Reaching the end of the car, the Shack was joined by Cracker, clinging to his brake iron, the two men looking back up train, then down at the tracks trailing off beneath the car, accelerating, no sign of the tramp, the train now moving too fast for any man to board. The Shack looked off at the cornfield clearly housing the tramp once again, nodded, satisfied, left the Cracker to drop down to the platform at the rear of the caboose where he disappeared inside. Turning, the Shack headed back up train, unseeing a hatch on the stock car, covered by a transom at the end of the roof. It was ajar.

Inside the empty stock car, a hay box directly below the hatch was stuffed with straw, feed for cattle in transit. Filtered light playing through the slatted sides of the car fell on the straw—and A-No. 1. The chicken still clutched in his hand, he waited out the sound of the Shack's boots retreating overhead.

Atop the reefer, the Shack was about to move onto the next car forward, half glanced back, stopped cold, eyes wide at what he saw.

Inside the stock car, A-No. 1 cushioned the straw to his satisfaction, settled back for a comfortable ride—when it caught him, his muscles taut as steel as he saw the transom above him starting to rise.

Flattening himself against the far wall, A-No. 1 waited, unable to do otherwise. A figure dove through the transom, fell to the straw. A-No. 1 sprung. A violent struggle, A-No. 1 grabbing the intruder, spinning him around, hand on his throat. Cigaret! A-No. 1 shoved the boy away, headed fast for the latch. Too late. The transom was slammed closed.

Atop the stock car, the Shack shoved home the iron bolt, locking the transom. Satisfaction on his face, he rose, moved back up train.

Inside the stock car, his face as black as the approaching night, A-No. 1 said nothing. But his stare told the boy what he'd entered. Wordlessly, he lowered himself to the straw, chicken still clutched in his hand, eyes low-lidded, piercing.

The sky red and black with the last light of day, engine '19', head-lamp on, drove off a turn, trailing the mixed train eastward.

Inside the stock car, light fading, Cigaret kicked furiously at the overhead transom. He had been at it awhile and, though the transom squeaked, it was stubborn.

Across the loft, A-No. 1 watched, stoic, an unlit cigar in his mouth, the chicken forever in his clutch. Collapsing on the straw, Cigaret glared. But not with that much confidence. No longer were the odds six to one. And the blood on A-No. 1's neck was an ugly goring.

"Who you callin' a fool?" the boy hurled at the older tramp.

A-No. 1's face didn't change. Nor did his position. He continued to gaze.

"See here, you call me a fool I'll push your face in for you!" the rant went on.

Cigaret waited for the rage that was madness, for lips flecked with soapy froth. It wasn't what he saw. Calm and impassive, A-No. 1 stared, seemingly lost in a great curiosity. It unnerved the boy. Coming off the straw, he threw himself at the left side door, then across the car at the right, then across the car again against the left, the doors holding fast when he heard a hollow roar. The train was moving onto a trestle. It was crossing a river, and slowing. Ahead, through the dip and rise of the trailing smoke through the slats of the stock car, were the lights of Sidney, Nebraska.

Cigaret collapsed to the floor of the car in a fit of despair.

"I guess I'd like to get hold of that Shack's throat," he wailed. "I'm tellin' you the truth, I'd squeeze it, take my tip for that!"

A sudden burst of light. Cigaret started half out of his skin. A-No. 1 had lit a match. He stared, incredulous.

"You ain't goin' to light up in here!?"

A-No. 1 ignored the question, lit his cigar, took a deep drag on it and the flame flared up.

"You'll burn us down!"

"Makes no diff, kid," the older tramp answered, waving out the match. "We're gone, no doubt about it, what's comin' in here."

A chill ran through Cigaret.

"It's nothin' but an old pig car," he said, looking about.

"Pigs eat corn. That's hay."

"Well, it's nothin' but an old steer car," the boy replied.

"So long, kid. If you croak first I'll pray for you."

"Don't get huffy with me! Let me tell you somethin'—what do you *mean* so long?"

"They'll be loading steers in here up at Kearney."

"Well, what of it?"

"Steers got horns, kid. Big ones, too."

"Well, what of that?"

"You ain't got any."

Cigaret gawked as A-No. 1 smoothed out a section of hay, lay back in seeming resignation.

"Ain' cher never heard of kicking at steers?" But there was panic in his voice. "Of scarin' 'em plenty? I'll holler, call for a cop, that's what!"

"That's ninety days on the rocks."

"'Ninety days on the rocks' ain't the horns."

"It ain't the rocks either, not in this part of the country, and it ain't ninety days. You're paroled to the bottom of a slew while the Sheriff pockets two bucks a day for your keep. That ain't a ghost story, kid. Two bucks a day's a lot of bread. Even the law's sweating hard times. Country's gone to hell."

Oh, for a Stew Bum sitting there. Or an Alkee Stiff or Dub. Cigaret had bit into prime. Grasping at a treasured weapon, he trusted his life to it, his mouth.

"They couldn't get away with it."

"Why not?"

"You remember Heehaw Mike, all right," the boy blustered.

"The old time Yegg?"

"I ain't trying' to scare you. You ain't seen Mike around, I guess."

"Heard he died of a broken neck in Texas," A-No. 1 nodded.

"You heard right."

"You're the one chilled Mike?" A-No. l answered, seemingly impressed.

"Now you know me," the boy said with swagger.

"How was Texas?"

"It's still there, so's he," Cigaret answered, thrown by the question.

A-No. l nodded. "Heehaw Mike got it in Frisco, shot full of holes by nobody knows."

Cigaret burned from humiliation, his little red eyes swimming wildly about as A-No. l pulled another match from his coat. His cigar had gone out. He lit the match.

"I won't leave you to face it alone, kid," A-No. l said. "We'll die game. You understand?" Holding the match to his cigar, he puffed till it smoked. "Them horns won't take us alive."

He tossed the still lit match onto the straw. It exploded into flames.

Cigaret couldn't believe his eyes, leaped for the straw to stamp out the fire. A-No. l backhanded him, sending him hard against the side if the car, the boy's eyes wide as the older tramp gathered more straw from the floor of the car, threw it on the fire, went for more and heaped it too as Cigaret scampered for the far end of the car, whirled, incredulous to see A-No. l throw his cigar atop the blaze.

In the engine cab, the Shack warmed a cup of coffee with steaming water from the escape valve. Across the cab, the Hogger eased back a notch on his throttle bar, his head out the side window measuring his approach to Sidney. Closing off the fire box, the Coaly turned to the tender, jammed his shovel into the coal. His eyes went suddenly wide as he looked down train.

"Cap'n! Lawd, Jesus!"

Moving fast up onto the gangway, the post between the locomotive and its tender, the Shack started over cars. The stock car at the rear of the train trailed plumes of smoke.

In the caboose a lantern gave light. Refilling his tin with coffee from a pot atop a wood burning stove, the Cracker climbed back to his perch in the cupola, a glassed-in enclosure protruding above the roof from which he could watch and see that the train was running smoothly. Easing onto the seat, he looked back toward the engine, and gawked. The Shack was pounding down train over rooftops.

The Cracker could not understand. He saw nothing wrong. Turning he glanced out at the rear of the train, and started half out of his skin. The trailing stock car was wild with smoke. Flames were lapping through its slatted sides.

The Cracker dropped from the cupola to the floor of the car, moved out onto the platform at the rear of the caboose. Grabbing the end ladder leading to the roof of the trailing stock car, the Cracker scrambled up, came off the ladder, moved fast down roof toward the transom.

In the stock car, A-No. 1 was like Belial at a cremation. Leaping up and down, he fanned the flames, hat in one hand, chicken in the other. Behind him, pressed against the rear wall of the car, Cigaret, too appalled for words or action, cowered in fear.

On the roof of the stock car, the Cracker worked futilely to wrest open the transom. The shack entered fast, grabbed the Cracker, hurled him back, all but throwing him off the train. Ripping back the bolt, he threw open the covering. Flames leaped from below, driving him back.

In the Sidney's Dispatcher's office overlooking the rail yards, a Yard Clerk pounded in to spread the news.

"Fire on the '19'!" he shouted.

But the bespectacled Dispatcher had already seen it. Pushing away from the window, he headed down the staircase into the yards where a Yardlet, Yardman, and Yardman's Helper were already crossing tracks as they held on the sight of the train racing toward the yards, a dragon with its tail on fire.

In the engine cab, the Hogger disengaged the throttle bar, spun the brake valve. The sound of air cutting in moved rapidly down train, a series of pops. The drivers spun wildly, then caught, began to ease the train back.

In the stock car, the grabbing of brakes flattened Cigaret against the end of the car wall. Hanging to the door post, A-No. 1 pulled himself forward, dove across the car into the flames and through the charred and fire-weakened slats, emerged through them, tumbled over and down the bank of a culvert, coated with ash and dead cinders. The chicken, freed from his grasp in the fall, was off, cackling through the yards.

Up track, a Groundhog, a switchman, raced for the turnout, grabbed the switch bar as the train rolled past, wheels chattering on the cross tracks, its heavy brakes showering sparks like pinwheels. But the switch bar was unyielding. And the flaming stock car was not ten yards away. The Shack came off the side of the caboose, pushed the Groundhog out of the way, grabbed the switch bar, bent it fully.

In the engine cab, the Hogger, watching out his side widow needed no orders. He opened he brake valve, pulled the gear lever into reverse, engaged the throttle bar. The drivers spun wildly, then caught and began to ease the train back onto the turnout. The stock car, flames leaping higher and higher, backed onto the turnout leading off the main and into classification yards.

Between the caboose and the stock car, the Cracker worked frantically to pull the coupling pin as the Shack reboarded, grabbed the pin with both hands, pulled it free, moved instantly off, waving, shouting forward as he hit the ground, his words lost in the roar of the flames.

In the engine cab, the Coaly saw the signal, turned to the Hogger. The old engineer pushed the gear lever forward, gave full throttle, the squeal and screech of the drivers enough to split ears. The stock car disengaged from the caboose, continued alone down the classification track.

Inside the flaming stock car, Cigaret looked about, terrified, sensing the free roll of the car. Instinct dictated survival. He dove through the fire and out through the charred slats, hit the gravel beside the track. A bruising roll that cut and skinned, he came onto all fours in time to see the stock car. Half flames, half railroad car, it careened down the last hundred feet of the classification track and smashed into a concrete termination bumper at the end of the rails in a shower of fire and flaming wood. Cigaret tried to scramble to his feet. Not fast enough. Strong hands grabbed him, spun him about, Cigaret staring up at the Yardman and the Yardman's Helper, two astounded, disbelieving faces.

On the opposite side of the train, the Shack raced toward the stock car, did not break stride, headed into the flames as others gathered. Switchman and Yardlet. The Dispatcher and Yard Clerk. The Cracker pushed through, headed into the fire after the Shack.

Inside the flaming stock car, the Shack searched frantically for some sign of the tramp. The Cracker tried to assist, but the flames were too intense, driving both men out, the Cracker falling to the ground on all fours, coughing hideously.

Stumbling to a barrel of water fed by a hand pump, the Shack dropped his head into it, held it there, pulled his head free, resting his weight on the lip of the barrel, arms extended, palms down, his back to the growing crowd. A low growl boiled up from deep within the Shack's throat.

"Who greased those journal boxes?"

He turned, sharply. Behind him yard hands high-stepped about in a worry of something to do as the stock car burned to a skeleton. The immediate gathering, including the Cracker, stood transfixed. The Shack glared at the Yardlet.

"When I pick up an empty, it's not going up cause some damn Yardlet forgot to pack an *axle* box!"

The Yardlet's face turned crimson. His mouth opened to protest, but the Shack pushed off the barrel, unpossessed of conscience or moral instinct.

"Clean those housings, oil and repack bearings, wedges. You ever hand me another fire—!"

"That's not what happened," the Yardlet protested.

"It never happens again!"

The Yardlet, whose name was Leach, bulged with fury. But the Shack's face, inches from the Yardlet's, was savage with rage. The Yardlet swallowed. He nodded. It would never happen again.

The Shack turned. The crowd parted. More than parted, gave him berth as he headed across tracks toward the Dispatcher's Office as the fire truck, bell clanging, raced onto scene, the fire team off and into action, hosing water onto the flaming car with little result. The Yardlet's voice, when he spoke, was low and hoarse with outrage. He indicted the Shack as he had never been indicted before, particularly now that he was safely out of hearing.

"Pig! I'll fix him right! So help me, God! Why don' he come back?"

The Yardman Helper entered fast, grabbed the Yardlet's arm, the Yardlet pulling it away, humiliated, furious.

"Get your Goddamn hands—!"

"What do you want for Christmas, Leach?" the Yardman Helper said with wild excitement.

"Damn his soul to hell!"

"What else? Of all you could have, Leach?" He spun the Yardlet about. "The one thing never been done. A tramp haulin' that son of a bitch off his high almighty! A bastard hobo ridin' his train!"

"Never happen."

"It has!"

2

THE ENGINE SHOP AT THE REAR OF THE ROUNDHOUSE,
illuminated by overhead lanterns, was a great wide shed. Clouds of
dust and metal filings danced in lantern light. The floor was cluttered
with headlamps, brass engine trimmings, flat wheels, and dismem-
bered boilers. Usually the place was full of snorting power, hammer-
ing and grunts and shouts of men wrestling with crippled hulks and
engine parts. Not now. Now everybody was watching Cigaret propped
against the lower end of a huge pile of sand. Nearby a large round
stove was splashed cherry red with heat, coffee boiling in a pot atop it.
The Yardman and Groundhog hovered above Cigaret. The Yardman's
Helper joined them, then the Yardlet. All stared down at him. Cigaret
stared back, one to the other, not sure what he was into.

"Look, any you fellows Baptists? My old man's a Baptist. I'm trying to get home, he's dying."

The Groundhog broke their silence.

"You're goin' for a year on the rocks."

"Stick you!"

"*Two* years—"

"How'd you make that train?" the Yardlet asked.

"Like any other," Cigaret shrugged.

"The '19' ain't like any other."

"A local."

The Groundhog's face turned crimson.

"You lying little beggar!"

"Ain't you heard of the Shack?" It was the Yardman's Helper. "The '19' belongs to him."

Cigaret stared, at four very tense expectant faces. What this was all about he did not understand, only that he was very much the center of focus. The Groundhog was chewing a quid, jaws working quickly.

"I'll take a chaw off that plug," Cigaret nodded at it.

"You ain't going to live through the night," the Groundhog answered.

"Give it to him," the Yardlet said.

The plug was handed to Cigaret. He bit off a chaw.

"It was easy."

He paused. They were hanging on every word, their eyes ablaze with expectation.

"I was waitin' for the flyin' mail when this ratty ol' freight comes off the curve, slows down track to pick up an empty."

Quick side glances between the four yardmen. The Yardlet edged closer.

"Say, you boys know the rule out at Mary's if you ever hit Denver?" Cigaret stalled, trying to get a fix on where to take this. "I guess she'd take you in anyhow, but most of the blokes when they goes out there—"

"Come on, come on!" The Yardlet snapped his fingers.

"I'd just laid down to pound my ear when I hear someone pushin' away to beat the devil and I look out and here's this Shack, long hair flyin'. Course I was curious, so I jump on to give the big man a stare in the face. You can figure we didn't gab much. He's wavin' this hammer and swearin' like a big-ass—"

"Bull shit!" the Groundhog cut in. But his disbelief was beginning to waver.

"Go on!" the Yardlet pushed the boy.

The bit in his mouth, Cigaret did just that.

"So I just ditched him and settled down in the empty, till this sorry lookin' 'bo comes draggin' through the transom, got us both locked in, the old fool, so I had to burn my way out. He's cinders now, you can bet."

He stopped, stared from one to the other. He didn't know if he'd pulled it off, or what he'd pulled off if he had, but he was ready to keep on trying. Wet showed on the faces of the trainmen, glistening in the silence. The Yardman's Helper was the first to move. He backed away, wildly excited, snapping his fingers at the Yardlet.

"Leach, you're gonna get a Christmas present in July!"

"Damn, let's put it to him!"

"What time's '19' pull out?" The Yardman's voice was hoarse with excitement.

"Six in the morning. Bound east for Omaha!"

Everyone was into it. Even the Groundhog now. "I ain't missin' this. I been waitin' for years!"

The Yardlet and the Groundhog bolted out the door. The Yardman turned to Cigaret.

"There's a party waitin' for you," he said.

Cigaret's mouth parted in wonder. He stared at the Yardman.

"No tramp rides the Shack. It ain't never been done."

Eyes wide and dancing with firelight, the boy looked from one to the other.

"You lookin' at the man," he chortled, swelling with importance.

Reaching down, the Yardman grabbed Cigaret by the collar, hauled him to his feet.

"This one's good for a twenty!"

With the Yardman's Helper in tow, Cigaret was led from the shed, headed toward unimagined glories, the shop left to its jumble of inert machinery—when a sudden trickle of sand played down from above. A Yegg, a roving criminal of trampdom, sat high atop the sand pile, lost in darkness. He was young, no more than twenty-five, black eyes, flat blond face, and broken nose. He wore an Army hat which sat on the back of his head. His shirt was open, disclosing an American eagle tattooed on his chest. In his hands, he held a jug of corn liquor. For a moment, he did not move, then slid down the sand to the floor of the shop, sat there, charged by what he'd heard. Rising, he clutched his beltless pants, moved out fast.

A hobo jungle clung to the edge a running brook, pitched awkwardly, haphazardly in a thick strip of woods off the Sidney rail yards.

A half dozen fires burned, fifty to forty feet from each other, each with its separate cluster of hoboes working over them like Army cooks. Some hauled water from the creek while others peeled potatoes or prepared scrappings for skillets. Still others stood on rocks in the brook, washing themselves. Rags and clothing of every size and color stretched on a wire from one tree to another. Rude little make-believe, scrap wood and tar paper huts stood near each other at the edge of the trees. They had three sides and a roof, the fourth side open. Everywhere were men, or what remained of men. But there was a buzz through the camp unlike any in memory. It was an undulating wave, from one camp fire to the next. Some said it was true. Some said it *couldn't* be true. The Shack had been boarded and *ridden*? Who did it? Who *could* do it? To a man they knew the answer to that. And they knew he'd be coming.

At the entrance to the jungle, a pile of debris was scattered and heaped, odd junk from generations of tramps and trains. Chunks of billboards, the relic of an upright piano, cuspidors, garbage cans, slop buckets, a bar stool. Surplus from the war two decades earlier formed a hut amid the debris. Newspaper and comics from Teddy Roosevelt to Jean Harlow and Alley Oop were plastered to its sides, protection against the night air. Black tarp, cut to fit the irregular architecture of the roof, faced the sky.

At the mouth of the hut, comfortably dozing in the folds of a de-wheeled baby carriage, was Smile, a five foot six ex-clown. He was sixty, looked eighty, had been there longer than the debris.

"Smile?"

The aging tramp's eyes fluttered open. Bruised and covered with soot and cinders, A-No. 1 emerged from the night.

"A-No. 1!"

"How they hangin'?"

"Still there, last I looked."

"That's the good stuff."

"I *heard* you was comin'," Smile said, a grin spreading his semi-toothless face. "Boys have it you tried the Shack, rode in on '19."

"Twenty miles in an empty ain't tryin' him. That's coppin' a feel."

"Still A-No. 1," Smile said with awe and admiration.

Pulling the newspaper from his hip pocket, A-No. l dropped it in the older man's lap. Smile saw what it was, checked the date on it.

"Only a week old," he beamed. "You are a sweet thinkin', fast trackin' man."

He rose, placed the paper on top of a stack of dated Journals, pulp and movie magazines, looked down at A-No. l's boots.

"Your boots are shot."

"Lost my kit to some road kids," A-No. l answered.

"I got an extra."

A-No. l stepped into Smile's hut, found them, checked the size against his own, found they'd do, hung them by their strings around his neck and came back out.

"Shack hurt ya?"

A-No. l grinned a tight grin.

"Don't laugh at the devil," Smile warned.

"I ain't laughin.'"

"Why don't you settle like me. I've talked with F.D.R., fought with Pershing, slept with Harlow, tamed the tiger, seen the elephant and gone over the falls. I been on the road and with it and never moved more than a foot."

"That ain't a question."

"It's got an answer."

There was a pause, the bond of intellect and intelligence between these two above other 'bos.

"Let's go among 'em," Smile advised.

They moved into the jungle, tramps rising, falling silent at the sight of A-No. l, in awe of him, which they readily would admit to, afraid of him which they would not. For he was the aristocrat, Tramp Royal, the primordial nobleman of the road, daring where lesser men only dreamt, going it alone, sharing nothing. Stew Bums, Alkee Stiffs, Fakirs; Shovel Bums, Gay Cats, Mushers, miserable men, the shabby tricksters of life, too desperate to look at the stars, they waited breathlessly for some morsel of acknowledgment, or recognition, or word of his exploit if true.

He reached a fire, six or seven 'bos about it. One was a Stew Bum, a dreg of vagrantdom. He wore a black satin shirt and a greasy blue neck tie and leered through a mouth that sagged at one corner where a crimson scar led downward from his lower lip. Another was a Fakir, an umbrella mender who learned his trade in prison, a decrepit middle-aged hobo who wore a black moustache and several days growth of beard, his collar yellow and black and much too large, his few remaining teeth snagged and crooked. They were working over a Mulligan Stew.

"Open up you Stew bums, Alkee Stiffs," Smile led off. "You think you're on the road? He come in on the '19'. A-No. 1!"

The Stew Bum could not contain himself.

"Did you get close to him?"

Plunging his hand into the stew, A-No. 1 pulled out a piece of meat.

"If you get close, they say, he'll throw you under the wheels," said the Fakir.

"K.C. Red went under," the Stew Bum added. "And a lot of other blokes."

"Some say nine."

"Sixteen."

"Some say more."

"How close you get?" the Stew Bum pressed.

A-No. 1 licked his fingers, nodded approval.

"Good grub."

"Bummed the whole country for what we didn't buy," the Fakir beamed.

"What you didn't buy is good," A-No. 1 acknowledged.

An Alkee Stiff moved in, and a Gay Cat.

"Did he take you to the deck?" The Gay Cat asked. "Did he use his hammer?"

He was one-eyed, pants torn and ragged. The 'bos looked quickly to each other. It's what they all wanted to hear. A-No. 1 nodded at the pants.

"Where'd you bag 'em, the Rescue Mission? They cheated you, 'bo. The Jesus shouters saw You comin'."

He moved on to a nearby fire, hoboes trailing. There was little there of value, mostly old men. One was Gink, an occasional laborer. He wore a shapeless hat with no band on it, his mouth puckered up as if he were continually blowing on hot soup. Another was Peg, a gnome-like little hobo who carried a crutch, the shoe of his amputated foot tied around his neck. Eagerly he addressed A-No. 1 as he entered.

"Do you remember me?"

The shoe, not the tramp, took A-No. 1's eye.

"That time out of Kearney," Peg went on, "we loosed them cars on that trestle and all the sheep went into the drink?"

"Not dead, Uncle?" A-No. 1 nodded, recalling. "I never thought you'd live through the summer."

"Did he use the chains?" asked the Gink. "Did he put the steam on you?"

"This sort of bummin' ain't like old times," the Fakir shook his head. "They got bummin' down and gouged it."

"He goes in the morning, son of bitch." It was the Stew Bum, always flushed to bring the latest rumor or news. "Omaha. It's posted."

"Good riddance," Peg answered, almost a growl.

"I met him once on the deck."

His name was Shine, a colored vagabond. A powerful man in a dirty purple undershirt and dangling suspenders.

"'Bos said don't do it. He laid me out like I weren't even real."

"Keep the engine to your back when you're decked," A-No. 1 counseled. "You won't take cinders in your face that way. Your feet, if they go out from under you, you're into your man, the deck won't throw you away."

"What do you think it is, your birthday?"

A-No. 1 turned. So did everyone else. It was the Yegg from the engine shop.

"He beat the Shack!" Peg said. "Rode the empty in on '19."

"The hell he did," the Yegg gloated. "A punk kid beat the Shack. They got him down in Dispatch." He nodded t A-No. 1 "He screwed it up."

The tramps were thunderstruck. None more so than A-No. 1. His face was positively fiendish, so malignantly did he stare at the Yegg. Plunging his hand toward the fire, he pulled out a flaming ember. The Yegg bounded backwards, fell, but was quick to his feet.

"He carries a knife!" Peg warned.

"You ain't tellin' him somethin' he don't know," Smile whispered.

Clearly something terrible was about to happen. All eyes were on A-No. l, expressions dumb and bewildered, so stunned were the 'bos by the indictment. Ember in hand, A-No. l sauntered toward the Yegg. The Yegg tried to hold ground. But his face became convulsed and white. What approached was annihilation. He backed off, hand fumbling for his knife. But he was not A-No. l's target. Passing the Yegg, A-No. l moved to the edge of the jungle, stared out at the water tower looming above the yards.

In the jungle the 'bos sensed what was about to happen. It moved through them like a wave, wild stirrings of life. Alive with revolt they watched as A-No. l slapped out the flaming ember on the side of his trouser leg, carried it down the embankment, away from the jungle, into the yards, marched through them, across tracks, the firelight from the still burning stock car playing on his face, yardmen, forever frantically working the fire, running past him, ignoring him, none noticing.

"What's he doin'?" asked Peg, incredulous.

"He's going for the glyph," Smile answered.

At the water tower, A-No. l started up the wooden ladder, measured steps, reached the tower catwalk. Groupings of names and dates and hieroglyphics occupied the face of the tower, a regular bulletin board where tramps exchanged information of their comings and goings. Turning to the tower facing, A-No. 1 scrawled quickly with the charcoal end of his burnt ember, then threw the stick away. On the tower he'd written:

"A-No. l. B.E. Omaha, 19. 10/24/31"

3

THE DISPATCHER'S OFFICE, THE BRAINS OF THE YARD, was a second-story low-ceilinged room, separated by a railing and low-swinging gate from an ante-room, the 'bull pen'. Before the windows overlooking the yards was a bank of rail switching controls. A door opened into a tiny telegraph office. A Telegraph Operator worked over the key, sending passenger and freight train orders down the line. A door opened into the 'bull pen' from outside stairs.

Before a large wall map of Nebraska, the Shack and the Dispatcher, both with tins of coffee, reviewed the rail line featured prominently entering Sidney from the west, then running eastward across Nebraska along the Platte River, through Ogallala, North Platte, Kearney, Grand Island, Columbus, Fremont, and into Omaha.

The Yard Clerk, poring over ledgers, looked up from his desk at a blast of chill autumn air. In the open door stood the Yardlet and Yardman's Helper, faces flushed, their eyes afire.

"This ain't a barn," the Shack admonished.

Across the bull pen, a pot-bellied stove spread heat. The Yardlet gestured at it.

"Any bitch if we—?"

The Yardman's Helper closed the door.

"Damn cold night."

The Yard Clerk returned to his ledgers, giving tacit approval. Battling to conceal their excitement, the Yardlet and Yardman's Helper crossed to the stove, professing interest in nothing more than achieving some warmth, spread their hands to the fire as the Dispatcher and Shack went about their business.

"Take on water at Ogallala," the Dispatcher advised. "North Platte, Kearney, setouts here along the river."

"You got a wheel report for my Hogger?" Shack asked.

"Nothing direct, unless something comes over the wire."

"What's my time to Omaha?"

"Twenty-eight hours," the Dispatcher said. "In by eleven in the morning if you stay on the advertised."

Through the door winged the Cracker.

"Engine's got a leaky flue," he called across to Shack.

"This ain't a barn!" the Yard Clerk scolded.

"Hogger's dusting her out in the roundhouse," the Cracker said as he kicked the door closed. "He'll have her hot and ready on the nose."

The Yardlet and the Yardman's Helper had the moment they'd been waiting for. Devious in the hands of accomplished con men, con men they were.

"Nobody?" asked the Yardman's Helper.

"Nobody," the Yardlet replied.

"Somebody."

"Who?"

"Skysail Jack, he made it."

"Your *butt* he made it."

"Sure, he made it."

"Ask him," the Yardlet answered, turning to the Cracker.

"What?" Forever eager at being consulted, the Cracker puffed with importance.

"Tell him if Skysail Jack ever rode Shack's train," the Yardlet said.

"In a coffin," the Cracker answered.

"Well, Vancouver Ned could make it," the Yardman's Helper insisted.

"Not even out of the yards."

"Chi Slim—"

"A musher."

"Chi Slim ain't no musher," the Yardman's Helper insisted. "He held down the Illinois Central."

"The Illinois Central ain't Shack's train."

"Well, somebody can do it," the Yardman's Helper insisted.

Feigning exasperation, the Yardlet appealed to the Cracker. Of such stuff were spider webs made.

"Tell him."

"Oklahoma Red, he tried it," the Cracker told them, in his element. "Know where they found him?"

"Where?"

"Which part of him?"

"Every train can be beat, that's all," said the Yardman's Helper, seeming to remain outrageously stubborn.

"Not Shack's."

"No more'n you can whip Jack Dempsey," the Yardlet said.

It had reached the moment for the coup de grace. The Yardlet pulled a bill from his pocket, slammed it down on the railing.

"Five says there ain't."

The Yardman's Helper pulled a bill from *his* pocket.

"Ten says there is."

The Cracker pulled out two tens.

"Match it or eat it!"

Suddenly, his wrist was encased in an iron grip, freezing the twenty in his fingers. A startled wince of pain, he looked up at Shack. The dark, sun-bronzed face had gone black, eyes ablaze, no clearness in them as he understood.

The roundhouse was located directly off the switching yards. An engine house for servicing locomotives, it was an asbestos-ridden circular building, poorly lit, with hoists and heavy machinery capable of major repairs, along with blacksmith and shop facilities. In the middle of an immense turntable sat Shack's locomotive, '19', mechanics there to complete repairs. But none were on the job, drawn, as were a growing group of others, to an unexpected, unheard of spectacle.

Seated in a cane-backed chair, leaning back, one leg draped over an arm rest, a smoke dangling from his mouth, Cigaret was holding court. He was having the time of his life. Cocky, arrogant, loving the attention, he held them enrapt with inventions of his exploits.

"If you're a thief and playin' the beggar, you'll end up with nothin', a warden's punk. Be an aristocrat of the rails or else what I calls bankrupt. Don't listen to none of them punks that tells you different, muckin' around, endin' up a Gay Cat or a Fakir. I knows this business. Don't know who knows it better—"

The door burst open revealing the Shack. He stood there, staring in at Cigaret, the Cracker behind him. So was the Yardlet and Yardman's Helper. The Shack did not take his eyes from the boy. He crossed, seated himself on a small turned around chair ten feet away. Total silence, the Shack on Cigaret, Cigaret on the Shack, the Shack's arms resting on the backrest of the chair. He pulled a watch from his vest, looked at it, lifted his eyebrows in reproach to the mechanics that no work was being done on his engine. The mechanics scampered to obey as the Shack looked back at the boy.

"You'll want an extra man," the Yardlet prodded.

"I got my crew," Shack answered.

"Just tryin' to see you don't take on company."

The Shack's chin came up on the line. Excitement boiled through the round house. The Dispatcher entered, stopped at the sight.

"I don't take company," the Shack replied. "Not even you, if you don't got a ticket."

His eyes swung back to Cigaret. So did everyone else's, breathless, waiting. The boy was center stage. It was narcotic. Wet glistened on his face. He manufactured a glare at Shack.

"Who you lookin' at, mister? I learned my trade on a tough road, that's a fact."

"You're not a 'bo," Shack virtually growled in contempt.

"Hell I ain't!"

"Talk up, lad," the Yardlet cut in, unable to contain himself. "Tell him."

"I can knock out any hook comes 'round." Cigaret tried to hold his ground.

"He beat it in on '19," the Yardlet blurted out. "He bought himself a free ride!"

The Yardlet was three yards from the Shack, nine feet, as the Shack left his chair, an avalanche of fury that the Yardlet strived vainly to ward off. He threw up one meaty arm to protect the stomach, the other his head, but the Shack's fist drove midway between with crushing impact. The Yardlet's breath expelled in a scream as he dropped. Cigaret was half out of his chair, but the Shack was on him, hands on either side of the arm rests, caging the boy to his chair.

"Do you know what I do to people who say what you've done?"

"I did it!" The boy was shaking but defiant. "I rode your goddamn train!"

The Shack's hand shot out, gripped Cigaret by the biceps of one arm. The boy had steeled himself for it, determined to brazen it out. But the enormous strength of the man was too much. He wilted, but would not shriek.

"Where you from kid, ditching the nuns? What're you trying to get 'em to think?"

Cigaret sat, his muscles refusing their duty, so great was the pain. Shack lifted Cigaret's chair, slammed it down hard, breaking its legs, Cigaret tumbling to the floor.

The Dispatcher started forward in protest.

"Shack."

The Shack recovered himself. A lucid gleam came into his eyes. He released his hold with a short contemptuous bark of a laugh.

"Only one tramp's got the balls to try me and that ain't you. You're nothing but a lousy little bum. You better own up to that or I got a job for you down by the river."

The Yard Clerk exploded into the round house. "A-No. 1! His name's on the tower they're sayin'!" For the moment, he couldn't find voice. "He come in on '19', and he's takin' it out! Bound east, Omaha!"

About the room, awe. The Dispatcher pulled off his glasses. The Groundhog and Yardman's Helper looked up from assisting the Yardlet. A Machinist's Helper looked about, revealing his sixteen years of knowledge, bewildered, not understanding.

"A-No. 1. Who's A-No. 1?"

The Cracker had not moved. He did now. His eyes swung around, wide and white. The others followed his gaze, looked toward the Shack. The expression on his face never changing, he continued to stare down at Cigaret. The boy didn't know what to do, what move he should make. Shack pulled slowly back from the chair, ignored him, crossed to the stove, poured himself a tin of coffee, swirled the liquid about, took a swallow, thought a moment. A smile crept out of him, but he quickly killed it.

"Never met him," the Shack replied. And he was gone.

The Yardman's Helper broke the silence.

"He makes it."

"He don't" said the Groundhog.

"He goes all the way."

"400 miles?"

"If he gets through the day into the night."

The Yardman's Helper grabbed the Yard Clerk by the scruff of his shirt.

"Get the Telegraph Op on his wire!"

"You're crazy," the Groundhog roared.

"He's got a chance if there's fog," the Yardman offered.

"Tell 'em in Ogallala what they got comin'," the Yardman's Helper continued to the Yard Clerk. "Tell 'em in North Platte, Kearney, Columbus. Tell 'em to send it down the line."

The Yard Clerk looked from to the other. The Yardman's Helper catapulted from the Round House.

"Into the yards at Omaha!" the Yardman pounced, producing a fistful of bills. "Fade it!"

The Cracker brings his hand down with assurance. It holds a twenty out to the Yardman.

"That's one sucker he'd like to meet."

He looks toward Cigaret with a smirk. He was gone.

IN THE SIDNEY JUNGLE A-NO. 1 SLEPT in the open next to Smile's hut. A bottle of whiskey, a pot of stale cold coffee, his new shoes, mirror, straight edge lay near him. A fairly new blanket half covered him. It was the best of what the 'bos had to offer, not much, but the best of it. Smile slept soundly in his hut, the others by their fires which were embers now.

Cigaret eased from the woods, rubbing his arm painfully bruised by the Shack, took measure of A-No. 1, which was all he dared take. Chest swelling as though he were about to say something, Cigaret gave up on it, slumped to the ground thirty feet away, back against a tree, forearms draped over his knees. He tried to hold it, he couldn't. His head dropping down between his knees, he tried to ignore the growls of hunger in his stomach.

Sensing his presence, A-No. 1 awakened, rolled over, looked at the boy. Whatever was in the older tramp's mind, he revealed none of it, rose, picked up a tin, and strolled to the creek. Reaching it, A-No. 1 dipped his tin into the water. If Cigaret thought the drink was for him, he was mistaken as A-No. 1 drained the cup.

"Hear you beat the Shack to hell," A-No. 1 said finally, staring off into the night.

"You're A-No. 1, ain't cher?" Cigaret said.

A-No. 1 said nothing.

"Well I'll be jiggered. Why, you haven't forgotten that time in Austin—"

"You're in pretty poor country, kid."

"I've changed a little, I know—"

"You're up a tree, you better know it."

Cigaret gave up the bluffing. His tone when he spoke betrayed his awe.

"They say you're ridin' him out in the morning," he said.

"He hurt ya?"

"He tried."

"Hear you been tellin' the yard you made a sad ass of him."

"I kidded him good," Cigaret answered returning to bluster.

"How's that?"

"I did!" Then with bravado, "He knows nothin'."

"Fight him, beat him, kill him if you can. But don't ever figure him stupid."

"He's shit."

"Is he?" said A-No. 1, "What would you be without him?"

A long moment before Cigaret answered, then, "What would you?"

A-No. 1 looked Cigaret over, sensed the boy's hunger, the strain at the leash. He dug into his pocket, pulled out a half-eaten Baby Ruth bar, tossed it to him. Cigaret grabbed for it, then hesitated, looked hard at A-No. 1.

"I ain't beggin' from you," he said.

A-No. 1 ignored the remark, returned to his dirt bed, lay down to recapture sleep. Cigaret bit into the bar, finishing it in a gulp, then sagged into a despairing crouch, head down. Minutes passed, four minutes, five. Slowly Cigaret lifted his head. The look on his face was not defeat. He swallowed, licked what chocolate remained on his lips. He looked at A-No. 1. His shoulders squared.

Nothing but pre-dawn mist as engine '19' backed it's tender off a turnout onto a makeup track, the Cracker riding out the bumper. A tug of resistance as in the engine cab, the Hogger closed the brake valve, Coaly feeding the firebox. Sharp, spitting exhausts of air sounded from open cylinder cocks. Quickly speed lessened, then the collision, the tender coupling with the waiting cars. The Cracker dropped in the coupling pin, connected the brake hose. The Hogger cut in the air, a quick chain of gasps down train.

In the yard, it was nearing six o'clock in the morning, and the train was made up and all the yardmen had come to watch. Grease-balls, Muhops, Dingers, Ash Eaters, Gaffers, drawn by word of the duel—the Shack who could beat any tramp riding out against A-No. 1, the primordial nobleman of the road. And not a man whose pulse did not quicken at the thought, conflicting though it was, of the tramp emerging victorious.

In the caboose, illuminated by a kerosene wall lamp, the Shack inserted two gloved fingers inside the globe of an unlit lantern, twist-ed the glass around and around till it was shiny. Dumping oil in the fount, he set the lamp on his desk and lit the 'bug'. On the base of the lamp, painted in large white numbers was '19'. The Cracker boarded, entered carrying his lantern already lit, waited while the Shack at-tached the globe to his. The lantern glowed red.

Crossing to a locker, the Shack opened it, one of several various-ly located, providing for the storage of heavy supplies: chains, journal brasses, knuckle pins, rerailing frogs, and wrecking tools for emer-gencies; signal fuses, torpedoes, signal flags, and lanterns, all stored as neatly and ready for instant availability as the flags and code books on the bridge of an ocean liner.

Replacing the fuel oil on its shelf, the Shack took down his ham-mer, four pounds of shiny forged steel, slipped it into his belt. Then he took down a torpedo, a warning charge set to explode when crushed by the weight of a wheel. He picked up his lantern, turned to exit, the Cracker following him out.

Emerging into the early morning mist, the Shack and the Crack-er moved forward along the length of the train, each on one side, checking doors and couplings, under bracings and handrails, run-ning lights and truss rods. Nothing escaped their notice, the Yard-men glued to the Shack's every movement.

The train had been largely remade. Following the engine and tender, it consisted of eight cars: reefer, gondola, box car, stock car, flat car piled high with lumber, a second box car, roof covered hop-per, caboose. As the Yardmen watched silently, the Shack reached the second box car, went underneath, gave the gunnel a tug, one of two longitudinal truss rods that ran the length of either side of the car.

For a moment, he speculated, then moved on as the Cracker boarded between cars at the down train end of the second box car. An end ladder climbed to the roof. It was secured to the framing by half inch lag screws, three inches in length. The Cracker grabbed the ladder, pulled with slight force, enough to reveal that the screws had been loosened.

Reaching the tender, the Shack looked back at the rear of his train over sounds of the air pump racing, charging the line. The blower, opened slightly to raise the smoke, grumbled mildly. The Cracker raced up train, came across the down train end of the tender, rejoined the Shack. Turning, the Shack looked forward, followed the engine's head lamp, its white finger of light flattening against the mist. He handed the Cracker the torpedo. The Cracker ran with it, ahead of the train.

The Shack moved forward to the front of the engine, past silhouetted clusters of Yardmen, who wondered at his emotion. Up track, some 200 yards ahead of the engine, the Cracker knelt by the rails, attached the torpedo. Rising, he ran back toward the train.

At the turnout leading off the spur, the Switchman stood waiting with the Dispatcher who held the train's orders. The Shack approached, staring back at his train, then fixedly up track. Visibility was variable, 100 to 200 feet, a ground fog low and clinging. The Cracker ran up to the Shack, nodded that all was ready. With an answering nod of his own, the Shack indicated the Cracker was to take up his post. With little more than a break in stride, the Cracker ran back toward the caboose. The Shack turned to the Dispatcher, hand extended for the train orders. The Dispatcher was not happy with what he perceived was occurring, held onto the orders.

"You got your work cut out," he said. "There's a fast mail coming through the Junction in twenty minutes."

"I'll be there in ten," the Shack answered.

"Not at yard speed you won't."

"I won't be going yard speed," the Shack said. "I'm going to highball."

The Dispatcher pulled back, stunned.

"The hell, now just a minute—!"

"I'm not giving away nothing free in this fog!" the Shack answered. "I got 2,000 yards before I got to worry about the round house and cribs. I'll have 40 miles an hour under me. He wants to try and deck that he'll end up selling pencils!"

"You're not balling the jack out of *this* yard, not *my* yard," the Dispatcher grabbed Shack's arm, infuriated, "I'll give you the clip on how you go, by God, I'll telegraph division—!"

He broke off, pale, his hand quickly releasing its unauthorized grasp. The Shack's voice when he spoke was controlled but emphatic.

"Telegraph division, brains. Tell them you want that tramp on their road."

The Dispatcher wilted. The Shack pulled the papers from his hand, moved back toward the engine.

In the engine cab, the Coaly had returned to feeding the fire, the Hogger releasing the air as the Shack climbed aboard. Handing the man at the throttle his written orders, the Shack looked down at his watch.

"5:59," he said.

The orders fastened to a clip above and forward of his driver's seat, the Hogger adjusted his time piece, a man about sixty, whose sole ambition was to get his engine through the following day, fearing, somehow, the day the engine went, so would he.

"Five fifty-nine," he acknowledged, looking up.

He stopped, aware that the Shack was measuring him. The Shack turned to the Coaly. The Negro fireman glistened with sweat, closed the fire door.

"She's ready to run, Cap?"

There were not many Blacks who'd made it into the White man's work-a-day world. Coaly was one. He had no intention of losing it. The Shack reached overhead, gave the whistle two long blasts. The Hogger pushed the gear lever forward. His left hand depressed the throttle bar. The engine leaned her weight against the resistance of the trailing cars and snorted gently, then angrily as the wheels began to roll.

At the turnout ahead, the Groundhog's lantern rose and fell, the signal clear to go.

In the engine cab, the Shack climbed up and stood on the gangway, stared up over cars toward the rear of the train, seeing three or four in the mist, no more. Quitting the gangway, the Shack moved in behind the Hogger, peered out the engineer's window, up track, saw only fog.

At the turnout, the cars rolled by: reefer, gondola, box car, stock car, flat car, second box car, hopper, caboose, trailing the engine off the spur, speed 8 miles an hour. As the caboose cleared the turnout, the engine's lead wheels crossed the torpedo, exploding it, notifying the crew that the train had cleared the spur.

In the engine's cab, the Shack reacted to the explosion, pulled away from the window, opened the throttle till it rested against the last peg. Instantly the engine trembled and shook from the vibration of its drivers, the train lurching forward. Startled, the Hogger grabbed for the throttle, but the Shack held it firm.

"Keep it open!" he ordered.

Shovel poised mid-air, the Coaly stared, agape.

"You'll burst her cylinders!" the Hogger panicked.

"All she'll take!" the Shack hollered. Then to the Coaly, "Keep your eyes on that steam! Two forty!"

Climbing fast to the gangway, the Hogger stared up over the engine, at the stack belching fire, looked down at the right side drivers, pounding, the cylinder packings beginning to smoke. Dropping back into the cab he turned to the Shack.

"She's old!" the Hogger pleaded. "She ought to be in the hospital! Her cylinder packings are wearing through, and her right side rod is pounding!"

Hanging out the cab window as far as he dared, his fist locked on the throttle, the Shack watched the track ahead, the fog and rails racing by as the engine drove across a series of cross tracks, headed into a curve, the Hogger and Coaly terrified as the Shack cut in air, the engine threatening to leave the rails. It didn't, it straightened, the Shack cutting off the air as the train came off the turn, headed into a straightaway, racing clearly too fast for any man to board, as a caution sign flashed by, a fixed marker:

" JUNCTION – TWO MILES"

Ahead, between the Kearney yards and the Junction was a turn-out, a 'business track' off the main, used for storing cars. In the fog, Smile, surrounded by a group of fixedly watching 'bos, knelt before the switch stand working on the key lock with lock picking tools. There was a soft click from within the mechanism. Smile pulled back, nodded up at A-No. 1 emerging from the mist. Moving past the 'bos, A-No. 1 reached the switch stand, ran his fingers together, grabbed the switch bar, bent it. It gave, as easily as a prostitute's virtue.

Aboard the cab of '19', the old engine had survived. The sound of her pounding rod had diminished. The stack no longer belched fire, but smoke. A second marker flashed by:

"JUNCTION – ONE MILE"

The Shack looked at his pocket watch, nodded, satisfied. The Coaly closed the fire door. The Hogger started to climb onto his seat. He never made it. A sudden lurching of the engine slammed him hard against the wall of the cab. The Shack, too. And Coaly, who was almost thrown from the cab as the engine drove onto the turnout, leading it off the main onto the "business track," three stored cars coming up fast. The Shack, the first to recover, grabbed the throttle bar, hauled back on it, pulled the gear lever into neutral.

"Air! Air! Cut in the air!" he shouted.

Clutching the brake valve, the Coaly opened it fully. The train's wheels screeched, smoke pouring from them as the Shack yanked the gear lever back, depressed the throttle totally. The engine's drivers reversed, steam cracking, popping as the train skidded on, the setouts looming large ahead.

"Sand!" the Shack shouted.

The Hogger, still dazed, grabbed the sand box arm, pulled hard to start a great grinding noise.

Sand spilling on the track in front of the drivers, speed quickly lessened, the engine sliding to a shivering, grating stop ten yards from the setouts, smoke pouring from every journal box. The Cracker was off the caboose virtually the moment the engine stopped, stood at the switch stand, staring stupidly. Half of the next to last car, the hopper, and all of the caboose still occupied the main line.

A mile ahead at the Junction, an interlocking system of tracks controlled by a tower, the single main line proceeded through, west to east. A feeder track swung in from the northeast, connecting west to the main at a turnout at the base of the tower. Eastbound traffic out of Sidney had to be past the junction along the single main track before westbound traffic entered off the feeder. Safety was dependent upon strict adherence to train orders and schedules, alertness, and quick thinking, all of which seemed strained to the limit by the Tower Switchman.

He stood at the turnout, peering tensely west along the main toward the expected east bound '19' out of Sidney, then northeast along the feeder and the anticipated west bound fast mail. From neither direction was there any sound. Only fog. Occasional patches of clearing from the rising sun permitted visibility of 500 feet. But swirls of mist followed quickly, lowering it to 100.

Lumbering to the tower, the Switchman climbed the outside ladder to the tower catwalk, turned to the railing, gripped it with large gnarled hands. Behind him, the Tower Operator emerged from his office, a room just big enough for a stove, desk, wall clock, chair, and not an oversized human being, along with a bank of levers connected by rods to the switches below. The Tower Operator glanced at the Switchman, eyes asking the question. The Switchman shrugged against the cold, stared bleakly up track.

"Nothing slow about '19,'" the Tower Operator said, acid in his voice.

"He ain't one to fool around," the Switchman answered. "You can bet he's making it up."

"He better," the Tower Operator said. "That fast mail's going to be blowing out plenty."

A mile west at the "business track," the Shack had come up beside the Cracker, was staring, incredulous, at the car and a half still on the main. When all at once there was something else. A cough? A laugh? He whirled, barely catching sight of a hobo's grinning face, pulling back into the fog. He turned, looked further into more grinning faces. Realization of what had happened, and how it had happened enraged him. The Cracker had pulled out his watch, was looking at it nervously.

"Six-five. Eleven minutes."

The Shack looked back at the cars still lagging on the main line, then up the main toward the fast approaching mail. He could kill. Turning, he high stepped back toward the engine over catcalling and whistling.

In the engine cab, both the Hogger and Coaly were dripping with sweat, the shock of their near disaster coursing through them. The Hogger tapped his steam gauge, examined the water glass.

"She's all right," he whispered, still shaking. "She's a good girl. I'll put her high-heeled slippers on, she'll take care of us."

When the Shack's voice cut through the mist.

"Pull her forward!" He pounded aboard. "You got the ass end back on the main!"

Over whoops and whistles, the Hogger leapt to obey, engaged the gear, opened the throttle, looked out the side of the cab as the engine eased forward toward the standing setouts. As the Shack moved from the right side of the cab to the left like a caged animal, the Hogger held the controls. His hands were shaking as the point of the engine collided with the first of the setouts, pushed the grouping, three in all, down track, ten feet, twenty. The lead set out came against the bumper at the end of the track, could go no further. The drivers of the engine spun uselessly, shut down.

The Shack was out the left side of the cab, moving back up track, past expectant, delighted hoboes, keeping distance, watching from the edge of the fog, no sign of A-No. 1. Reaching the switch stand with the Cracker, both men stared. Half of the last car, the caboose, still occupied the main line. The Cracker was sweating, and not from exertion as he glanced at his watch.

"Nine minutes."

Turning, the Shack ran fast back toward the engine.

In the engine cab, the Hogger cut off the air, increased the blower to maintain draft and heat on the blower as the Shack boarded.

"Back her off, she won't clear," he ordered.

He flipped up the cab seat, pulled out a rubber and canvas hose. The Hogger and the Coaly stared, no response to the order. The Shack leaped for the gear, engaged it, grabbed the Hogger's hand, slapped it onto the throttle bar. The engine pushed against the weight of its carry, began to reverse. Returning to the hose, the Shack secured it to the steam head atop the boiler.

The hose tied on, the Shack handed it to the Coaly, leaped off the left side of the cab, moved down train. The Coaly stared at the hose, realizing its intended use. He looked at the Hogger, then tried the hose. A stream of steam spit out.

Running with the reversing train, past silhouettes of taunting hoboes, spectators at a great event, the Shack reached the Cracker mid-train. In the Cracker's hand was a brake iron. No order needed, he knew what to do. Crossing over to the opposite side, the Cracker ran up track with the reversing cars.

Capturing the down train end of the tender, the Shack swung aboard as the train reversed. At the end of the flat car, mid-train, four down from the Shack, the Cracker boarded from the left side, crossed to the right, looked out, moved back again as the Shack grabbed a grab bar, swung out from his perch on the tender, looked up train, then down. Nothing. No sight nor sound of anyone other than the taunting 'bos.

Dissatisfied with his position, the Shack dropped back to the ground and ran past the reefer, then boarded, crossed to the right side, looked out, recrossed, looked up train. Nothing. No one. No A-No. 1

At the down train end of the flatcar, the Cracker recrossed again. Still nothing, as the reversing train had all but cleared the business track, was back on the main over the sound of air brakes cutting in.

The Shack ran to the switch stand, bent the switch bar as the engine cleared, closing the business track, reopening the freight train to the main.

In the engine cab, the Shack pounded onto the lower rung of the iron and stepped into the cab as the Coaly lifted the top gate of the tender to make coal more available. He was frightened. So was the Hogger.

"Cap, six minutes," the Hogger warned.

"Run her out!" the Shack ordered, grabbing a three foot length of chain off the back head.

The Hogger needed no further encouragement, depressed the throttle bar. The engine accelerated. The Shack dropped back to the ground, wrapping a foot of chain around his right fist, leaving two feet hanging down as the tender passed him.

Reboarding, the Cracker had climbed to the top of a box car, was moving over rooftops, searching, left side, right side, suddenly shouted.

"Shack! Left side! Left side!"

Whirling, the Shack saw him! A-No. 1! Bolting out of the fog, driving between cars. Instantly, the Shack moved to cross over. On the right side of the accelerating train, A-No. 1 ran forward. The Shack came off behind him, the length of chain flailing from his fist as he gave chase, A-No. 1 a car's length ahead, the train's speed increasing, threatening to match his own. Reaching the up train end of the reefer, the forward-most car attached to the tender, A-No. 1 boarded, between the two, started to cross, was driven back by a spray of live steam, the Coaly playing it from the canvas and rubber hose attached to the turret.

A-No. 1 clutched his arm, painfully seared. No time to deal with it, he started to recross to the right side, reacted to the Shack, closing, twenty feet, ten. Reaching for the grab iron on the up train end of the reefer, A-No. 1 took hold, slammed his foot hard on the step, swung his body onto the down train end of the tender as the length of chain in the Shack's hand swept down, a vicious arc that struck nothing but air as he boarded the reefer, stared in horror. Atop the down train end of the tender, A-No. 1 was spinning the brake wheel. The coupling between the tender and reefer separated. The air hose snapped.

Aboard the up train bumper of the reefer, the Shack was nearly pitched onto the track as the released air slammed on brakes of the reefer and trailing cars, the engine and tender pulling ahead, its cars left behind, A-No. 1 riding the engine and tender as they pulled away from the reefer and the rest of the train to the delight of the hoboes at the edge of the fog.

In the engine cab, the Hogger, realizing what had happen, fought panic, closed down the throttle as A-No. 1 was off and running up the right side of the tender.

Aboard the reefer, the Shack scrambled, released the brakes, quit the reefer to give chase to deriding catcalls as he tried to search out A-No. l, stopped, staring into nothing but fog, the tramp gone, disappeared. The engine was reversing past him, the Cracker hopping aboard the up train end of the reefer to secure the reconnection. For the first time, there was uncertainty on the Shack's face, in his voice.

"Hey! 'Bo!" He paused, then louder, "You listening?"

The Shack waited. A-No. l's image emerged from the fog, swirls of mist playing over his face.

"In three damn minutes," the Shack pleaded, "you're going to hear a whistle that'll be the Fast Mail comin' through the Junction. That means a head-on!"

"Sounds like a ghost story to me, Shack," A-No. l, answered with a chuckle of disdain, retreating into the fog. "See you around."

In the switching tower at the Junction a mile ahead, the Switchman stared at the wall clock, moved to the door, looked out. At the bank of controls, the Tower Operator pulled down hard on a lever, then shoved it back into upright, activating, reactivating the switches below, an impatient gesture as the war on his nerves was taking its toll. Turning, he glanced at the clock, and froze.

At the door, the Switchman had heard it, too: the shimmering tinkle of a washer or pin or loose connection, set vibrating by the distant action of wheels on rails. The Tower Operator paled. The Switchman moved fast out the door onto the tower catwalk, came up hard against the railing, listening, hearing nothing. He turned to the ladder, clamped his feet on either side of the ladder's upright supports, slid to the ground, the Tower Operator moving onto the catwalk, stopping at the railing, staring out.

At the turnout, the Switchman drew to a stop, stared in horror up the feeder track as it came, faint and unmistakable: the distant wail of a train whistle.

Down track, Engine '19' was reversing its tender, the Shack, still holding his chain, riding out the bumper as the Cracker pounded aboard. The tender and the reefer collided. Dropping in the tack pin, the Shack pushed off the tender, left the tying on of the brake hose to the Cracker, ran forward to the engine.

In the engine cab, the Coaly furiously scooped coal into the fire box. The Hogger engaged the gear in anticipation of the order as the Shack leapt aboard with a flailing gesture.

"Go! Go!"

The Hogger's gauntleted hand took hold of the throttle, and held there, frozen. Whirling, the Shack was about to vocalize the order—stopped, ears trained, along with the Coaly's, shovel poised.

Between cars, the Cracker turned, hearing it, too: the distant shriek of a train whistle.

In the engine cab, the Hogger panicked, slammed home the throttle. There was a terrible roar. The Shack grabbed the throttle, half closed it, opened the sander.

The engine quivered, smoke belching from her stack, exhaust barking. The drivers tried to bite the rails, spun uselessly, then took hold as its high-wheeling ceased. But the effort for the old girl was tremendous. Her exhaust became labored, its thundering boom reverberating against the fog.

In the engine cab, the Shack increased steam. The Hogger, falling apart, looked frantically out at the drivers.

"She's stalling! She's stalling!"

The Shack held the throttle bar firmly, looked fixedly out the driver's cab window at the stack belching smoke in thick black puffs and fire. The Coaly worked like a pendulum, transferring coal from tender to white-hot fire box when all at once the engine exploded ahead, its side rods pounding, hurling defiance.

A-No. l swept from the fog, drove in on the right side of the train, as the Cracker, boarding at the down train end of the hopper, caught sight of him heading for the down train end of the flat car, two cars up. Leaping to the ground, the Cracker took off for the flat car, made it to the stock car, one car down, but was no match for the acceleration of the train. Clutching the grab iron, he swung aboard the up train end of the flat car.

In the engine cab, the Shack, staring out the right side window, saw A-No. l board. His face contorted with fury, he moved to the left side window, back to the right. No choice, he was caught, committed, slammed his fist against the Hogger's gauntleted hand, pressed the throttle to the last notch, grabbed the whistle cord with his other, the whistle atop the engine pouring steam and sounding shrilly.

A half mile away, the fast mail roared down the feeder track, its own whistle announcing its approach to the Junction, its engine cutting through the fog, laying out a swirling wake of mist as down the main line engine '19' thundered eastward toward collision.

Leaping from the flat car to the first stock car, the Cracker searched both sides as he moved up train, seeing no sign of A-No. l, aboard or not, obsessed with not knowing as in the engine cab the Hogger's eyes were riveted on the track ahead, his right hand on the throttle bar, his left pumping the whistle cord.

On the hookup to the tender, the Shack stood, holding fast to a grab iron, leaned out, staring ahead. The fire door open, flames poured out. His ebony face wet with fear, the Coaly listened. He heard it: the sound of the incoming fast mail. Dropping his shovel, he turned to dive out of the cab. Coming off the tender, the Shack was on him, slamming his back against the backhead, when all at once the Hogger's sight out the right side widow cleared. A quarter mile ahead was the Junction.

On the tower catwalk at the Junction, the Tower Operator had seen the freight, frantically looked up the feeder track, fog clearing, smoke from the fast mail puffing over a ridge a third mile away.

In the engine cab of '19', objects raced by indistinguishably as the Shack held fast to the Coaly, the fireman limp with fear, the Hogger without will to do more than lock his hold on the throttle.

Atop the stock car, the Cracker stared in horror as the freight bore down on the turnout, hit it.

In the engine cab of the fast mail, the Engineer reacted, disbelieving at seeing the freight train crossing the intersection three hundred yards ahead. He pulled back on his throttle, cut in air and the emergency brake. There was the screech of metal on metal as the fast mail plowed on, no chance of stopping before the intersection.

On the Junction Tower, the Tower Operator grabbed the lever bar controlling the intersection, stared down at the freight train racing to clear the intersection from the onrushing fast mail. 100 yards separated the trains. Then 50. The caboose made it over. The Tower

Operator hauled on the lever. At the intersection, the rods activated, opening the main to the west bound feeder. The fast mail drove safely onto it, west, as the freight swept away, east up the main.

In the engine cab, the Shack ignored the Coaly and Hogger who had folded in exhaustion. Moving up over the tender he leapt to the roof of the reefer, moved down train over roofs against the buck and sway of the train, searching couplings and decks. At the up train end of the stock car, he met the Cracker who had worked his way back with the same result. Nothing. They look about, no sign of the tramp. But where? Did he fall, thrown to the side of the road? Or crushed under wheels?

"He ain't nowhere," the Cracker said at length.

Filled with doubt and silent speculation, the Shack wasn't sure.

"Check again," he ordered, and turning, moved back toward the head of the train. The Cracker held a moment, then turning himself, resumed his search down train toward the caboose.

5

ON THE LEFT SIDE REAR TRUCKS OF THE FLAT CAR, axels extended outward from the two wheels, each axel was capped by a journal box holding packing for lubricant to keep the axels from overheating. They were in size, about 4x7 inches and were spaced, from one wheel to another, about three feet apart. Clutching to the step, hanging down beside the trucks, his hips resting on the rear journal box, his heels on the forward one, was A-No. l.

It was not the best of all worlds. The journal boxes were hot. The road bed racing by was no more than a foot and a half below and the wheels kicked up pebbles and cinders. His feet were merely resting, the whole weight of his body supported by his arms. And the car was rolling and jolting.

Protruding from the bumper, best known as death woods, at the end of the flat car directly in back of his head was a grab iron. Squirming and twisting, A-No. l inched up till, with his right hand, his left clutching the step, he was able to reach up and above him, grab the grab iron. The next step was perilous. Drawing his feet up slowly, so that his left foot was resting on the rear journal box, he continued bringing his right foot to the end of the wheel, placed it firmly on the brake shoe. His left foot now joined the right. His left hand joined his right hand.

The grinding, clanking couplings securing the flat car to the second box car were directly by his right shoulder as he pulled himself up against the jerk and sway of the brake shoe, up onto the bumper of the flat car, left shoulder first, then left leg, then right, then pushing off the grab iron completely.

His work was not done. Open and exposed to any of the train crew crossing overhead, he had to find shelter. Stakes, secured in pockets attached to the outside framing of the flat car, held a two-foot-high board wall about the base of the lumber. The lumber itself, towering six to eight feet high, piled unevenly, and secured by ropes, offered an open area between the end wall and the butt ends of the lumber, the top of the lumber, longer pieces, extending overhead, concealing the pocket. With the last of his strength, A-No. l grabbed the top of the end wall, pulled himself over.

Dropping to the rough wooden bed of the flat car, breath searing his lungs, A-No. l rolled over onto his back, winced from pain at the searing on his shoulder from the steam hose, stared out at telegraph poles stepping by like a picket fence, their tops reflecting in the river alongside the track as the last of the mist was whipping away.

He wasn't alone. Across the open area, crouched against the butt ends of the lumber, as far lost in shadows as possible, Cigaret watched. How he'd managed to make it aboard, he'd achieved no bargain. Disaster stalked him in that great hairy red-haired form. He searched for deliverance. Out along the side of the car, maybe. There seemed to be a shelf, a foot wide, formed by boards. But his hat lay on the bed of the car, six feet away, by A-No. l's foot. His hand eased forward, inched toward the hat. His fingers ensnared it as the hairy red face came round, the eyes, a pair of open apertures, fixed on the boy.

Cigaret froze, arm fully extended, hand on his hat, as one would freeze finding a rattler coiled and ready to strike. A-No. l came to an elbow. Cigaret slammed back against the lumber, hat in hand, stared at the elder tramp. Red hair straggling over his forehead in a tangled mass of curls, A-No. l sat upright, measured the boy through narrowed eyes. Freeing his right arm from the right sleeve of his coat, revealing the red flannel prison shirt underneath, he pulled out his hand. In it was a closed straight razor.

Frantically, Cigaret searched for a weapon. An iron rod, a piece of board. With nothing but his own raw courage, he swung into a crouch across the open area, ready to battle with his fists. With a flick of his wrist, A-No. 1 snapped the razor open. Cigaret's eyes bulged at the sight, then stared in shock as A-No. 1 slid the razor across the deck of the car, the blade coming to rest at Cigaret's feet. Astounded, Cigaret watched as A-No. 1 unbuttoned the front of his shirt, peeled the left sleeve away, revealing the blistered, raw burn to his shoulder, back, and arm sustained from the steam hose.

"Get grease on that," A-No. 1 told him.

Scarlet worked through Cigaret's face. He'd been spoken to with an authority not meant for equals, dismissed as a tenderfoot, a green-horn. Outrage welled up within him.

"You want to pick one you got it!" he blustered.

Ignoring the boy, A-No. 1 reviewed his wounds. Taking the razor, Cigaret slammed his hat on his head, turned, seething, to the end wall, climbed it, dropped to the bumper. Grabbing the brake shaft protruding from the end of the flat car with his free hand, he swung low over the rear left side, reached toward the wheels. Excess grease oozed from the journal box. Scraping grease onto the flat of the razor, Cigaret suddenly lost his hat to the wind, made a desperate failed reach for it.

In the caboose, the Cracker occupied his perch on the cupola, eating lunch, a slab of pork between two dry pieces of bread, watching the retreating tracks. He had just inserted the sandwich into his mouth when he caught sight through the cupola window of Cigaret's hat, bounding back along the side of the rails. He blinked stupidly, sandwich clamped in his teeth as his head turned, following the flight of the hat. With sudden realization, his head snapped back.

In the open area between the end wall and the butt end of the overhanging lumber, Cigaret climbed back in from the bumper. Across the opening, A-No. 1 continued preoccupation with his wounds, held out his hand for the razor. Cigaret cocked his wrist, sent the razor sliding back across the deck in defiance. Hand extended, A-No. 1 stared, his mouth turned down, lips parted in a forbidding half-smile that registered no humor. Reaching down, he took up the razor, spread the grease on his burns. Scraping the razor clean on his pants, he closed it, slowly buttoned his shirt, Cigaret tensing, anticipating what his defiance had bought him, reacted to an unlikely sight. Pulling his own hat over his eyes, A-No. l, like a hairy red bear, huddled into the corner, curled up to sleep.

In the open area of the flat car, Cigaret dozed, the midday sun filtering through the lumber, throwing barred light on his face. An immense butterfly with brown and white wings lit on his head. There was total stillness. No wind. No sound. No movement. The train, unrealized by Cigaret, was standing motionless, half the cars midway across a timber truss bridge spanning the river flowing beneath the bridge fifty feet below when Cigaret was jolted awake by the train starting up.

The heat of unsatisfied sleep pressing on his brain, his eyes tried to focus, to orientate to his surroundings. He looked toward A-No. l, There was no A-No. l. His eyes opened wide as he came to his knees, looked wildly about. Nowhere was there a sign of the older tramp. Turning, he stared out over the side of the car, pulled back in shock at the drop to the river, all at once realized, the train was reversing. He looked back, out along the left side of the car toward the end of the train, pulled his head back sharply at what he saw, eased it carefully out, peered back again. At the down train end of the trestle, the Shack stood on firm ground, awaiting the reversing train. The caboose, the first to come off the trestle, rolled past him. Fighting panic, Cigaret worked his way across to the opposite side, looked back to see the Cracker standing directly across the track from the Shack, the train easing back between them, braking to a stop as the hopper, the next car from the caboose, cleared the trestle, the Cracker instantly boarding.

Cigaret fell back immobilized, the rapid fire of his heart beating, a trip hammer in his throat. It was a car by car search. Pulling a smoke from his pocket, he put it between his lips, but did not light it, sat there, swallowing panic, then moved, no indecision, pushed off the lumber, climbed the end wall, onto the bumper, saw the Cracker was involved with the hopper, grabbed the brake shaft, dropped to the ties atop the bridge. Clutching the guard rail running along the outside edge, he swung down through the opening between the ends of the ties and the top of the bridge, lowered himself into the bowels of the bridge beneath the overhead ties, track, and train.

Grabbing a wooden diagonal, he headed lower, too quickly. The drop of his weight like a sack of free falling sand, pulled his hands brutally down the length of the diagonal till his feet broke his fall on the bottom cord of the bridge. Unmindful of the splinters from the edges of the diagonal, Cigaret glanced back over his shoulder. Had they seen him? If they had he knew what it could mean. Trading the wooden diagonals for rusting metal hangers spaced alternately every ten feet, he moved forward along the cord, toward the up train end of the trestle, past stock car, first box car, gondola and reefer, the timbers groaning and popping from the prolonged dead weight of the train overhead.

He'd reached the tender when his left shoe wedged between the bottom cord and a slanting diagonal. He yanked his foot out. It came. Not the shoe. Holding onto a hanger, he reached for the shoe, found it stubborn, then freed it just as the engine's drivers reversed overhead. The vibration nearly bucking him from his perch, Cigaret grabbed for support, his shoe falling to the river below as he held, both arms wrapped about the hanger. The engine, backing another car off the trestle, crossed above showering steam. A jet of hot oil laced Cigaret's face. The sound of air brakes cracked through the train, the engine squealing to a stop directly above, the roar of its air pump and blower, the whine of its generator turbine resounding through the hollow of the truss bridge as though inside a drum.

The flat car has been backed off the trestle, the train again stopped. The Shack was up and aboard, climbing down over the wood. The Cracker who had gone underneath emerged, frustrated, having found nothing.

"Well?" the Shack glared.

The Cracker's shoulders fell. "Nothing."

"Damn right nothing. You never *seen* nothing."

"I did."

"A hat. A Goddamn hat!"

"Comin' off a car, goin' past."

"A rag. Some axel packing."

"Naw. Shit."

"A Goddamn newspaper, that's what you saw!"

"Maybe... hell—"

"What?"

"I don't know."

"Something or nothing! Which did you see?"

The Cracker shook his head, finally convinced. "Nothin."

"Bullshit, nothing! You saw a Goddamn hat!"

Half blinded from the oil, further panicked by noise and fear of detection, his left foot bare, Cigaret had been plunging on, hand over hand, the diagonals and hangers tearing at his hands and clothes, till reaching the up train end of the trestle, he came out onto ground, did not stop, not even to look back. His legs a pair of pistons despite one foot bare, he pounded through the open, along the incline, running parallel to and below the track, into shrubs and through them, the incline all at once littered with refuse: cans, a ripped up mattress, glass and broken crockery. His bare foot betraying him on a discarded pail, he toppled, head over tails, came to rest at the base of an incline, flat out, face down in a pile of dead ashes.

"By God," Cigaret heard the all too familiar voice, "there used to be a day when a dump had quality."

Ashes clinging to the oil on his forehead, hair and cheeks, Cigaret stared. Before him stood A-No. 1 in the middle of the dump, regarding the pickings with disgust. Of considerable size, enough to service a community, it was fed by rail cars discharging unwanted loads and trash down over the incline from the track forty feet above. Scattered wisps of smoke curled up from the relics of smoldering tires, a sofa, discarded clothing, bundles of newspapers, railroad and industrial waste. He stood near an abundance of discarded gallon cans, one of which he held in his hand.

"You didn't like what you found," A-No. 1 was going on. "Sell it to the Salvation Army for a jug of barleycorn as long as you looked 'em right in the eye." He shook his head at the sad state of affairs, discarded the can. "Trash has gone to hell in his country."

Cigaret had found a shoe, a size too large, he didn't care, slipped it on his bare foot. A low growl boiled up out of him. He came onto all fours.

"Get up out of that, you red-faced devil," he ordered.

A-No. l looked left and right, as though to see to whom the boy was speaking. Touching his fingers to his chest as though in inquiry, 'Who, me?' his eyebrows arched in mock surprise.

"Leavin' me to get mussed up. Stand up, I've got it in for you," Cigaret challenged.

"A regular out'n outer?"

"Watch out," the boy warned.

"To the finish?"

"Look spry!"

"Drive away."

Oh, for a Stew Bum standing there. An Alkee Stiff or a Dub. Cigaret had bit into prime. Grasping at a treasured weapon. he trusted his life to it. His mouth.

"You remember Heehaw Mike, all right," he blustered.

"The old time Yegg?"

"I ain't trying to scare you. You ain't seen Mike around, I guess."

"Did Mike croak down there in Texas dead certain?"

"That's it."

"There was a mean old bummer."

"That's the way to put it."

"You're the one chilled Mike?"

"Now you know me."

"How *was* Texas?"

"It's been there years," Cigaret answered, thrown by the question. "Everybody knows that. It's still there."

A-No. l nodded. .

"Heehaw Mike got in Frisco, shot full of holes by nobody knows."

Turning, he clomped through the rubble toward the incline. Cigaret held on all fours, burning from humiliation.

"You ever ride the Cannonball on the Wabash?" he bawled after the retreating tramp. "Come up on the C & A on the K.C.? Wait'll you hit the Pennsy, no tanks, take water on the fly!"

Reaching the base of the incline, A-No. l started up. Frenzy edged into Cigaret's face.

"No, wait a min, listen!"

Hands raw and bleeding, he started after A-No. l.

"We got an errand for us. We'll give 'em something to read about. Take the train and break his neck! Who knows this business better'n we do!"

On the incline, A-No. 1 stopped, looked back sharply, Cigaret falling forward onto hands and knees.

"This track ain't no place for you, kid. Walk on into the next town, beg a ticket out. Hit the French country, Montreal. You rub your stomach and the nuns'll give you a slice of sow-belly and a chunk of dry punk and let you sleep with the mules."

Turning, A-No. 1 continued up. The inference triggered Cigaret totally.

"I bummed this country years!" the boy raged. I got pinched in El Paso with Frisco Slim! Rode the White Mail out of Chi with Cincy Red!" He dug into his hip pocket, pulled out a two-inch piece of chalk, exhibited it fiercely. "I got my moniker on towers from Seattle to Mobile."

Plowing one foot after the other through the loose ash and refuse, A-No. 1 moved on toward the top, mindless of the noise behind him.

"I got fights with Syracuse Shine in Toledo," Cigaret blustered on. "Come over the hill with Sailor Boy full-fledged."

Clawing at the dirt, Cigaret started up the incline. A-No. 1 whirled. He stood a third way from the top, Cigaret a third way from the bottom. All ploy was gone from A-No. 1, all ease.

"You ain't stopping at this hotel, not my hotel!" he warned. "The stars at night, I put 'em there. I know Rockyfeller. I'm a great friend of Mark Twain. I know the Presidents, all of 'em. I goes where I damn well please, the President of the New York Central can't do it better. *My* road, kid. I don't give lessons, I don't take partners, I don't take students. Your ass don't ride this train."

His foot snaked out, kicked over a blackened five-foot length of circular tile, the broken off top of a chimney. Hollow and two feet thick it rolled, down over the incline, setting up a landslide of ashes, loose dirt and rubble.

Cigaret took the avalanche full force, the tile and rubble driving him back as A-No. 1 scrambled toward the track. Recovering, Cigaret started up the incline again, hands and knees over refuse, the sound of engine '19' puffing up to speed.

At the lip of the incline, A-No. 1 looked over the edge down track. The old engine was coming off the trestle, climbing, but losing no time. Sparks flew from her stack as Cigaret, hands and feet like pistons, drove for the top where A-No. 1 crouched, glanced up track to gauge the run he would have to make. It was an uphill ascent. The engine bellowed past. The roar she made as she crashed over he rails told she'd be a tough one to nail. The tender passed. The reefer and the gondola. The up train end of the first box car came abreast. A-No. 1 made his move, headed out as Cigaret gained the top of the incline.

Sprinting forward, A-No. 1 angled in on the stock car as it approached, his speed and that of the train nearly equaled. Reaching it he suddenly stooped, reached under the car, seized the forward gunnel, at the same instant lifted his feet from the ground, swung his body under the car, brought his feet to rest on the brake-beam.

In the engine cab, the Shack had seen it, turned fast to the backhead, grabbed a coil of bell-cord and a coupling pin.

Underneath the stock car, A-No. 1 worked hand over hand, hauled himself in. Between the top of the truck and the bottom of the car was a narrow space, barely sufficient to admit a man's body. A-No. 1 squeezed through it. Beneath him was the revolving axel, which he dared not touch. The wheels whirled, inches from his shoulder. Removing the 3x5-inch grooved pine board, his "ticket," from his pocket, he perched himself on the cross-rod, his bottom atop the "ticket," when, damn!

Cigaret was running alongside the stock car, trying to make it himself. His determination was fierce and he had good speed. He turned to go underneath.

"Not the gunnels, not the gunnels! A-No. 1 warned.

Cigaret went for the gunnel, clung for dear life, dirt and gravel flying, the ground flashing away beneath. With all the power bestowed by youth and fear, he pulled himself onto the cross-rod, perched painfully on the gunnel. But he'd made it, beat the '19', exulted in his conquest!

Perched on the cross-rod, A-No. 1 settled back against the cross-partition. He'd tried to warn. Woe to the tyro who took his seat on a gunnel. It was a lesson not long in coming.

Atop the first box car, the Shack grabbed the brake wheel at the down train end of the roof, swung down the end ladder to the coupling between the box car and the stock car. Straddling the coupling, one foot on the bumper of the box car, the other on the bumper of the stock car, he fastened the coupling pin to the bell cord, dropped the pin down to the track, played out the cord.

Beneath the stock car, the coupling pin struck the ties between the rails, rebounded with a metallic clank against the undercarriage of the car, again struck the ties. Cigaret saw what was happening. Terrified, he looked toward A-No. 1 holding his perch above the play of the cord, immune to the calamity, not even appearing to be stirred by it. Above, the Shack was playing the bell cord back and forth to one side and the other, the coupling pin given every opportunity to smash anything in its path, every blow freighted with death.

Desperately, Cigaret sought to fend it off. But he had no place to go, no place to hide. His hands were needed to hold himself to the gunnel as the pin hit him a glancing blow. Stoic, offering nothing, A-No. 1 watched as Cigaret was hit again, a cruel blow to the shoulder.

Straddling the coupling, the Shack had hit home, and he knew it. The train, increasing speed, lent deadly impact to the pin. He worked it vigorously, no longer playing out the cord, knowing he had the range.

Beneath the car, Cigaret's mouth flew open in pain. The pin had punctured his skin. Blood showed on his shoulder. Wind and dirt and gravel flew into his face, a good sized stone hitting his lips with such a rap that blood trickled down his chin, the coupling pin beating a veritable tattoo of death when all at once A-No. 1 reached out, grabbed the bell cord.

On the couplings between cars, the Shack was all but pulled from the train, so severe and unexpected was the jolt on the cord as beneath the car A-No. 1 hauled in on the cord, grabbed the coupling pin, looped it over the brake rod, tied it off. Removing his "ticket," he slipped it inside his coat pocket, grabbed the brake rod, eased himself out of the truck, down onto the gunnel.

The Shack yanked furiously on his bell cord. It would not give. With a violent oath, he discarded it, climbed to the roof of the stock car, raced down train toward the caboose.

Under the stock car, Cigaret saw A-No. 1 coming. Clinging to the gunnel for his life, he watched A-No. 1 circumvent the center cross tie, come onto the turnbuckle block mid-car. Grabbing the iron runner bar, the lower side door support, A-No. 1 pulled himself up onto the side of the stock car. Gaining a handhold in the next to lowest opening between slats, A-No. 1 secured his feet and left hand, reached down for the boy with his right. The boy was frozen, unwilling to move.

"Hand!" A-No. 1 shouted.

Cigaret shook his head, too frozen to do so.

"Grab it! It's got the chicken!"

Taking Cigaret's left hand, more grabbed than offered, A-No. 1 guided it to the step directly below the sliding door.

On the roof of the second box car, two cars down from the stock car, the Cracker had anticipated the Shack's need, came from the caboose to meet the Shack. In his hand was the Shack's hammer.

One the side of the stock car A-No. 1 reached for Cigaret's right hand, grabbed it, too, pulled the boy out and away from the gunnel. Feet only on the gunnel, A-No. 1's strong right arm boosted the boy upward to the door. Exhausted, bruised, and bleeding, Cigaret clung there, clutching slats. Exchanging his handhold on the slats himself for the grab iron by the door, A-No. 1 scowled in contempt.

"Cincy Red never taught you that."

A look of utter astonishment crossed A-No. 1's face as the grab iron, bolts previously, deliberately removed from the inside of the car, came loose in his hand. Frantically, he grabbed for the slats. He couldn't make it. The weight of his body pulled him away. He fell, down over the incline, ricocheting off tree stumps and rocks, disappeared into a hazel thicket crowding the river bed.

On the side of the stock car, Cigaret panicked. Desperately preoccupied with his own survival, he tried to swing back. Too late. The Shack had reached the end of the lumber piled high atop the flat car, the next car down. Without breaking stride, he flung his hammer. On the side of the box car, Cigaret brought his arm up to protect his head and face, the hammer barely grazing his shoulder, but causing his fingers to lose control of their grip. He dropped to the side of the roadway, tried to break his fall. The speed of the train was now too great. He stumbled along with the train, ten yards, twenty, feet churning, pitched forward, somersaulting down onto gravel and cinders and burnt grass outcropping the bank below the tracks as the train sailed past in a whirl of dust and trailing wind.

Gasping for air, chest heaving, lungs ready to burst, Cigaret stared at the sky, at clouds bulging upward, traveling in regiments of scattered wonder, when a great mountain of dark appeared suddenly, spreading across Cigaret's sight line like an ocean of ink. An intense darkness covered him, broken only by two tiny red stars that turned quickly into a pair of eyes. With a jolt, Cigaret sat upright, staring up at A-No. 1 squinting down at him through grease and grime and a welter of bruises. Lifting his head, A-No. 1 measured the train heading east and away. Without so much as a further glance at the boy, he turned, moved back down track away from Cigaret and the train.

Cigaret blinked in bewilderment, looked after the disappearing east-bound train, then at A-No. 1 plodding west, away, along the ties between rails, his movement unhurried but deliberate as he headed back where they came from. Slapping his hand alongside his pants, raising dust, Cigaret fought decision. Hating it, no other choice, he made it. He followed.

At 400 yards, a quarter mile, A-No. 1 suddenly turned off the tracks, hurtled over the side the incline. Reaching the older tramp's point of departure, Cigaret peered down from the edge of the incline, stared dumbfounded. A-No. 1 had returned to the dump. So confounded was the boy at what he was seeing he paid no attention to his precarious perch, the edge suddenly giving way, Cigaret tumbling head over heels, down the incline, to the rubble below where A-No. 1 was plowing toward a pile of discarded gallon cans.

Made of tin, as yet unrusted, with wire handles, they bore no labels. But they were what A-No. 1 was after. Picking one up, he looked inside it, threw it away, picked up another. Whatever he discovered in it satisfied him. He sailed it to the base of the incline, narrowly missing Cigaret's head, proceeded to investigate others, rejecting more than he accepted.

Cigaret hadn't the remotest idea what was happening, nor why. A fifth can dropped near him. A sixth and seventh as A-No. 1 continued his quest. Two more cans rejected, an eighth, ninth, and tenth were accepted, sailed after the rest. Crossing to the cans, A-No. 1 scooped up seven, the wire handles looped over his arms, looked back at Cigaret, nodded at the remaining three as though to say, "Well? Get after it." Turning, he started up the incline returning to the tracks.

Cigaret did not know what to make of it. The old fool had turned bughouse. Well, damned if he was going to be a part of it. He sat down hard, looked up after A-No. 1 regaining the tracks. He swallowed, drew a hand across his mouth, looked down at the ground, found a rusted iron spike. Wrapping his fingers about it, he dug away at the dirt, tension playing out, his eyes coming up again, looking after A-No. 1 who was heading west, away from the retreating train. Rather than tension releasing, it seemed to build. Cigaret's breath became more and more labored, the drives of the spike more vigorous as he seemed to become engaged in some enormous inner rage. But he had no options open to him other than one. A well of fury contorting his face, he brought his right hand back, sent the spike sailing. Rising, he scooped up the remaining three pails, no idea why, climbed from the dump back up the incline to the tracks, stopped at what he saw.

The tracks, unnoticed before by Cigaret, climbed steeply from the river through a gorge, spanned by an overpass. At the top of the grade, A-No. 1 sat beside the tracks, head down between his knees, catching his breath, his seven pails beside him. Cigaret staggered down track toward the older tramp, flopped disgustedly down on the ties ten yards up track from A-No. 1. Wet streamed down the boy's face. He swallowed against the spasms deep in his gut that cried out for water. His mouth was paste. But this was as far as he'd go.

A-No. 1 looked at the boy, Cigaret's eyes flashing defiance, rose, moved toward the youth. Cigaret tensed to meet him. His arm came up, finger extended in warning. A-No. 1's hand shot out, clamped about Cigaret's wrist, held it, then jammed it into the nearest pail, pulled it free. Cigaret's hand was coated with globs of black grease used for repacking journal boxes. A-No. 1 turned and began to apply the grease in Cigaret's hand to the rails.

"What the hell you doing?" the boy demanded.

"Teaching you."

"Why?"

"I'm still working on that."

It was forty minutes later that the prairie engine came off a turn, trailing its line of passenger coaches off the trestle. In the engine cab, the Engineer looked out his driver's side window. Ahead lay the climb up through the gorge. In the cab, the Engineer dropped his Johnson bar down a few notches and widened the throttle. The side rods danced as speed increased. The veteran engine shot ahead. Smoke belched from its stack as it hurled defiance at the climb.

In the engine cab, the Fireman was breaking up coal and scooping it into the fire box—when all at once the high wheeling ceased. The exhaust became laborious, thundered throughout the gorge. Speed began to dwindle. Startled, the Engineer grabbed the throttle, widened it. There was more steam, but big black puffs were coming out of the stack as speed slackened, even as the Fireman, his body working like a pendulum, transferred coal from tender to fire box, when suddenly a terrible roar! The engine's driving wheels had lost their grip on the rails and were spinning madly, finding no traction.

The Engineer closed the throttle. The spinning ceased. Again, he gave her steam. Almost at once, the exhaust became a grinding roar as the drivers spun uselessly. With a smothered oath, the Engineer shut her down, the train jolting to a stop on the steepest part of the grade. The Engineer bolted through the gangway, swung to the ground, the Fireman after him.

On the second coach, the door to the vestibule opened. The Conductor quickly descended. Leaving bewildered passengers leaning from windows trying to fathom what had occurred, the Conductor strode forward toward the engine. At the head of the engine, the Engineer and Fireman were down on the cinders as the Conductor reached them, his question answered before he could ask it as the Engineer scooped a handful of grease off the rail.

The Conductor's face screwed up in distaste. Haughty, well-dressed, with a beard and the dash of a militia colonel, he wore lilac kid-leather gloves. From his belt hung a gold-plated ticket punch. He was beside himself and he let the Engineer know it.

"We have a schedule to keep, Mr. Collard!" he said.

"Somebody greased the rails—"

"I don't give a shit! Get this *moving*!"

The Engineer rose, wiped the grease off on his pants.

"We'll have to double the hill," he said.

He turned back to his engine, the Fireman with him. The Conductor fixed the blame with disgust.

"Democrats."

The engine, separated from its cars, was backing down the grade. Traveling light, it had made it alone to the top of the gorge, spreading sand on the rails as it climbed, spreading more on as it descended toward its coaches waiting below at the base the grade. Recoupling solidly, its engine stood, breathing deeply.

In a clump of shrubbery Cigaret was alive with wild anticipation. His eyes were agleam and a short bark of laughter escaped him. A-No. 1 glanced at him, held on him as though measuring an idiot, looked back down track as the engine's great drive-wheels spun a few preliminary revolutions, then caught. The engine lunged forward, each car caught by the sudden jarring passed down in turn to the next trailing car in a rattling concatenation that shivered its way to the observation car. The train began to roll.

In the concealing shrubbery, Cigaret tried to contain his excitement, he couldn't, he started to make a premature dash for the approaching coaches. A-No. 1 grabbed him, hauled him back.

"Do what I do." His voice was flat, less warning than statement of fact. "Don't like it, just do it."

The engine and half the baggage car passed by. A-No. 1 darted out, Cigaret close at his heels. Two cars went by when A-No. 1 and Cigaret gained the train, fell into a steady trot beside it. Whatever A-No. 1 meant to do was not long in doubt. The fourth car slipped slowly past as they kept at the same even stride, uphill, moving faster as the train gained speed. The fifth car came abreast. A-No. 1 grabbed the handrail, vaulted lightly to the steps, and swung himself toward the vestibule that joined the fourth and fifth coaches leaving Cigaret to follow clumsily.

On the side of the coach, Cigaret had no idea what he was standing on, but soon found out. On the end of each car, suspended about eighteen inches above the level of the track, were iron stirrups, straddling the space between the two coaches, so placed that a workman might plant his feet in them and stand erect, albeit in a kind of awkward posture. There they both stood, in the stirrups, facing the vestibules, bracing themselves with the palms of their hands pressed flat against the glass panes of the windows in the enclosed ends of the coaches as the train drove upgrade through the gorge.

How long Cigaret could tolerate his position, he was beginning to more than wonder. His feet were trembling and his back was aching already from the strain. He looked down at the flying road bed. A-No. l's voice penetrated the roar of the train.

"Keep behind me. Watch your feet. Don't kick the glass out."

With that A-No. l placed his hand flat on the window ledges and drew up his feet from the stirrups to a place beside them. From a crouching posture, he rose and stood erect. His head was now on a level with the tops of the vestibules. As Cigaret watched, A-No. l planted his elbows on the sloping roofs that curved over the vestibules and muscled himself up.

Now it was Cigaret's turn. He stiffened his arms and swung his shaky feet to the window ledges as he had seen A-No. l do. He straightened his back gingerly, leading to the most desperate maneuver of all, did not give himself time to contemplate the peril of it, but, flinging his feet free of the ledges, launched himself into space, throwing his weight onto his arms, his elbows clamped precariously to the down-curving slope of the roofs, struggling frantically to hoist his body. It was at this moment that the train reached the top of the grade, whipped into a curve. The roof of one of the cars shot skyward. The other lurched downward. One of Cigaret's elbows slipped. He clawed, panic-stricken at the vestibules, kicked out wildly with his feet and heard his heel graze the window.

A-No. l's gnarled hand grabbed Cigaret by the collar, hauled him up, Cigaret's arms wrapping in a vice-like grip about a funnel protruding through the roof of the car. Two long rods ran the length of the roof. Unbuckling his belt, A-No. 1 passed one end of the belt under the rod and buckled up again, strapping himself securely to the roof. He lay down, his back to Cigaret. Wind streamed across the roof. Cinders flew like buckshot as Cigaret burrowed into the roof, clinging to the funnel to keep from being blown off as the train plunged eastward toward a battalion of dark clouds marching steadily up the sky. Seeking to Imitate A-No. 1, Cigaret reached for his belt to secure himself to the roof, stared in dismay. He wore no belt.

THE AGENT'S QUARTERS in the Kearney depot was cluttered with a small safe, lanterns with red and clear globes, red and white flags, hand held hoops for passing orders to engineers and conductors of moving trains, rate books, ticket stamps, sealing wax, brass seals, torches for melting wax, *Bullinger's Postal and Shipper's Guide* (both out of date), broom and duster. There was also a table with a telegraph, a wall clock, a chair with each leg set into the socket of a glass insulator in case of electrical storms, along with another chair not so protected for qualified callers. This was a day for it. Storm clouds were building and lighting split the sky in the distance. The telegraph key was chattering, the Station Agent, seated in the insulated chair, hovering over it, hurriedly writing down the message that was being sent.

Across the room, a glassless window looked into the depot waiting room, a half dozen off-duty trainmen crowding about the window at the sound of the key. They looked toward the Agent. His head came up, offered the one thing all had been waiting to hear: a quick, short nod. An Ash Eater pushed off fast, headed out.

In the crew room, where trainmen washed and changed their clothing and found coffee, the several present looked up, startled, as the Ash Eater showed fast in the door. Some were at basins, some were half dressed.

"Nineteen's coming into the yards at North Platte!" the Ash Eater exploded the news. "The Op's picking it up on the wire!"

The men dove for the door where others, drawn to the incoming message, poured from the roundhouse, shops, and switching yards.

In the Agent's quarters, three trainmen had squeezed in from the waiting room: a Dinger, a Switchman and Mudhop, breathlessly stood over the Agent. Completing his recording of the incoming message, the Agent rose, ripped off the message. Handing it to the Dinger, the Agent bolted out to spread the news.

"The Shack ditched him, whipped his ass!" the Dinger exploded as he read the note.

The Switchman and Mudhop grabbed the paper over the roar from the yard as word reached the trainmen.

"Coming up here like kings and flushes!"

"Paradin' around all stuck on hisself!"

"*That'll* teach those sons a bitches!"

The Kearney hobo jungle lay between the railroad embankment and the river. A stream ran through it down to the river. An empty box car on a siding offered protection against rain and a place to sleep. Under the shadow of big trees were dying campfires, around them shadows of hoboes, some sitting on the butts of logs, others on the ground. No one moved as they heard the celebration and knew its meaning. Each silently turned inward upon himself, hybrids and degenerates, their illusions of pride and self-respect so suddenly dashed. Even the young ones, recent dropouts from an unordered world, felt the loss. Overhead, the sky drew as leadened as their spirits.

6

A **BLINDING FLASH OF LIGHTENING STREAKED** through clouds that hid the sky, silhouetting the passenger train, smoke from its Prairie engine trailing low over its rain-soaked coaches. An explosion of thunder followed as the engine screeched over a crossing and in a moment was in open country again.

On the roof of the coach, Cigaret had no eyes for the wild beauty of the prairie. His thoughts were of survival as rain splattered on the roof like broken pearls. A wind whirled over the train that lurched through the wet, dark day as lightening flared again, turning the car roof to a glistening green.

Cigaret tried to shield himself from the windswept rain. He slipped, grabbed the rod running the length of the roof, returned to holding onto, gripping the funnel. Choosing rather to be lashed by rain than crawl across the wet and heaving roof, he made no further move. He looked toward A-No. 1 sleeping soundly, the cold air numbing Cigaret's muscles until a stupor fought to gain control of his brain. Silently, he struggled with a primitive lust for life, shook his head violently, pounding the car with one foot then the other to revive his ebbing circulation

All at once, no warning, he slipped, down over the side of the car to the track below, striking the roadway, his skull crushed into oblivion!

Atop the roof, Cigaret started in terror at the distorted fancies crowding his brain, desperately clung to the funnel.

"Don't listen to the wheels, kid," A-No. 1 was momentarily awake and admonishing, "less you're tied down and want to sleep. When your blood gets thick, edge over, take a look. It'll start flowin' again."

Cigaret listened for more, but there was no more as A-No. 1 returned to his berth. All the boy was aware of was a growing numbness again. He edged over, looked down at the wheels of the coach, churning and grinding, polished steel where they rode the rails, each a cutting edge, a liquidator.

Cigaret edged back fear as his blood flowed again. He clung to the funnel, his hair whipped like a wet rag, the whistle of the engine barely heard above the roar of the cars, the shrieking wind, and the mad patter of rain. He tried to fight the rhythm of the wheels, but they got to him slowly. His eyes began to close, suddenly came open hard as he heard it. A-No. 1 was snoring.

The Prairie engine, trailing its coaches, roared on, no slackening speed. The rain had stopped, the heavens steel gray and black, the sky completely hidden as Cigaret tried for sleep now, curled about the funnel when the shriek of the engine's whistle startled him awake. Hanging onto his anger, he stared at A-No. 1 still curled in apparent sleep, when he saw it! The freight train, not ten cars in length, standing on a siding, its heavy engine puffing like a tired horse. The Prairie engine roared past, its coaches and observation car a silver glitter and was gone, leaving the track open again to the freight train. Whirls of smoke coughing from its stack it crawled off the siding, back onto the main, an orange "19" on its nose and the side of its cab.

Bolting upright at the sight, Cigaret found A-No. 1's hand flattening him to the roof, the two tramps huddling low.

"Pretty sight, huh, kid?"

"We'll ride that bastard yet!" the boy squealed, elated.

"There's a *we* in that I ain't settled on," the older tramp replied, and laid back to finished his nap.

Kearney, Nebraska, mid-day, as the train entered, bell tolling. slowing through huddled low wooden houses breaking the plains, fields sweeping up to them, unprotected, gaunt frame shelters like grocery boxes. Only the grain elevator and two church steeples rose above the low lying mass.

Past the elevator, a storage tank, a creamery, and a lumber yard, onto Mercantile Street, a broad unenticing gash, the prairie let in on every side, steam pouring from escape valves as the Prairie engine continued to slow. The skeleton iron windmill on a farm a few blocks away hovered like the ribs of a dead buffalo over single story roof tops. Past Dunn's Billiards, the Kearney Hotel, a lunch counter, and bar.

With a great hiss of expiring vapor, the Prairie engine stopped before the depot, a squat red frame station, the platform sparsely littered with unadventurous people as drab as their houses, as flat as their fields.

On the roof of the coach, clothes drenched, A-No. 1 was up and off the side of the car opposite the station platform, swinging to ground from the vestibule stirrups. Instantly, Cigaret followed, wet to the bone, down the side of the coach, and suddenly froze halfway. Through the window in the brightly lit Pullman compartment, a woman, naked as Mother Eve, was taking a bath in a copper four-footed bath tub. She saw Cigaret, met his gaze. More in provocation than shock, she turned to him, taunting, exposing all when A-No. 1 grabbed him, hauled him off and under the coach.

Cigaret's mouth snapped open to protest. A-No. 1's hand was across it. It's then that Cigaret heard it: the tread of a heavy pair of feet in squeaky shoes approaching, nearer and nearer straight toward them.

Squeak. Squeak. Squeak.

They paused at Cigaret's head, enormous feet encased in brand new shoes sparkling with polished highlights. Above them, Cigaret caught a glimpse of trousers very blue and very official. Slowly, the knees bent, and Cigaret beheld the figure of a man sagging to a crouch. To immeasurable relief he was a Negro in a Red Cap, one of the station's Porters. And he was reaching out with eager fingers for a beautiful cigar butt fully five inches long which someone had evidently discarded after no more than a half dozen puffs. The Porter's eyes glistened as his fingers closed about the prize. His knees stiffened and he went squeaking away.

Ten seconds, twenty, A-No. 1 was out from under the car. For an instant, Cigaret didn't know what to do. Succumbing to preservation he chose the only course open to him, rolled out from under the car, streaked after A-No. 1.

A hundred feet from the train, a box car occupied a parallel track. Reaching it, A-No. 1. flattened against it, Cigaret following, both protected by shadows, the only sound the periodic breathing of the Prairie engine ejecting jets of excess steam. When another sound stopped A-No. 1 cold. His head turned sharply and stiffened. Neatly stacked to one side, awaiting storage and shipment aboard the box car, were a half dozen crates of turkeys. With the intensity of a bird dog, A-No. 1 stared back at the train blocking view from the station platform, turned his attention again to the turkeys.

Lowering to a crouch, A-No. 1 edged out from the shadows, crabbed his way toward the nearest crate, looked about. No one was within sight, all blocked by the train. Reaching up with scarred, calloused fingers he carefully removed the wooden peg that secured its gate, reached inside. A howl of panicked gobbling sent A-No. 1 recoiling, retreating to the protecting shadows of the box car next to Cigaret once again, when the shriek of the Prairie engine's whistle announced the train's departure.

Slowly pulling out, it left to A-No. 1's and Cigaret's view the depot platform, and more importantly full view from the depot across the now vacated tracks of the crated turkeys. While Baggage Men hauled sacks of mail inside the depot, a Policeman paced the platform, nightstick flipping back and forth in is hand.

A-No. 1 weighed the moment, trapped between compelling urges: jail or a dinner of prime grilled bird. He looked about for a means, and found it. A sack of corn stood just inside the box car. Reaching into his coat pocket, he pulled out his straight razor, flipped it open, sliced an eight inch wound in the sack. Corn spilled through.

Glancing over the top of the crates, A-No. 1 looked toward the depot again where the Policeman still paced. Pocketing the razor, he glanced at Cigaret watching, eyes as wide as saucers, A-No. 1 dug out a fistful of corn, turned to the boy.

"You up for this?"

"Whaaa?"

"Dribble the corn around the side of the car."

"Dribble."

"When one of 'em follows, grab him."

Cigaret swelled with excitement.

"I'll nail the sucker, break his neck, he'll know it!"

"I'll watch for the bull, let you know if he's comin'."

Cigaret reached for the corn. A-No. 1 pulled it back, assessing the boy.

"I'm trustin' you, kid."

Seemingly reluctant, but apparently with no recourse, A-No. 1 handed Cigaret the corn. Cigaret grabbed it, looked toward the depot, started into his mission. At the unlocked crate, a turkey picked up the scent. Butting open the unlocked gate, it flopped to the ground, began heading for the trail of corn Cigaret laid down around the corner of the standing box car. Safely concealed by the car, the boy dropped into a crouch, all business now, dreams of a massive roasted drumstick as he awaited the turkey's arrival… and waited… and waited… when all at once there was a wild flurry of squawking!

Stunned, Cigaret circled back about the end of the box car, reacted to the sight of the turkey swept from the ground by A-No. 1 on a dead run. Cigaret howled at the betrayal, started to give chase, found himself hauled back, his feet flying out from under him. The Policeman had circled behind the box car, grabbed Cigaret, his fingers buried inside Cigaret's tightly buttoned collar.

His instincts for survival instantaneous, Cigaret ducked his head under the Policeman's arm and began to rapidly twist. The Policeman screamed with each revolution as the delicate tendons in his fingers threatened to rupture, the muscles and nerves mashing and crushing together under the boy's collar. Desperately, he yanked his hand free, Cigaret off and running, the Policeman after him with an oath.

Arms and legs flapping, Cigaret descended down a culvert, the Policemen behind him, sliding down the incline, through the muck, night stick drawn, Cigaret losing him in a pocket of woods. Still the Policeman did not break stride. Plowing through trees, limbs slapping his face, he emerged from the woods, stopped cold as he found he'd burst into the heart of the Kearney hobo jungle.

The rain had come and gone, the mid-afternoon sun, played in through the trees, throwing checkered shade on a pool of water, every object drenched. A long abandoned track spur ran through the jungle off the yards terminating at the end of the encampment where the discarded stock car sat on rusting wheels. The clothes of the shivering tramps dripped with water as they rekindled fires, containers of every sort brought out to cook in: broken shovels and pie plates, empty tomato cans, soup kettles and soap dishes. There was no sign of Cigaret, but there were the hoboes, an instant transformation taking place at the sight of the Policeman and his sight of them as he glanced from one to the other. They were like beasts, penned together and showing their teeth, full of potency and wild stirrings of life, all eyes on the intruder.

A Pokey Stiff squatted in the mud. Flabby faced, black eyes, he wore a thick valise strip as a belt around his torn corduroy trousers. Beside him, a ragged overcoat lay open with a spread of dog meat partially wrapped in brown paper, a carrot that had been run over by a wagon wheel, and a sugar-bun with a mouthful bitten from it rescued from the gutter. His toes exposed through rags, he hungrily eyed the Policeman's shoes.

The Policeman swallowed. His ego gave way to pretense. He started to strut on, stopped as he saw a Grease Tail, the dreg of vagrantdom, peering above a growth of whiskers, gray and dirty, untrimmed for years. What was visible of his face looked as though it had, at some period in time, stopped a grenade. Coatless, he salivated over the Policeman's tunic. Beside him, a Halfy, one leg lost beneath the knee, no hat, bald head, sat by his crutch with the contents of a can of Sterno emptied into a dirty kerchief, squeezing it to extract the alcohol, covetously regarding the Policeman's hat. Wet broke out on the Policeman's face.

"Well, I guess he ain't here, all right," he said, voice cracking, betraying his fear.

He edged back toward the woods, trying to save face.

"You tell him it's ninety days on the rocks if I ever get my hands to him. He's sent up, it's that for sure."

It was at this precise moment he backed into great yawning jaws, cackling, gaping to pluck out his heart, talons flashing, wings closing to engulf him. Against the forces of Satan, he battled for his life, spun about and stared, at the turkey, head held down by A-No. l. The tramp's demeanor was ferocious, domineering. There seemed a lust in him, akin to madness, carnal hunger to the 'bos who quickly gathered, A-No. l playing to them to their delight, and there was nothing the Policeman could do about it.

"Send him up?" said A-No. l with utter disapproval. "Why I'm as surprised to hear you say

that if you was a preacher. His daddy's president of Standard Oil. He'd turn the Navy on this

town if you sent him over."

The Policeman affected a posture of authority, groped for the bird.

"Beat it out of here in the morning. I catch either one of you stiffs round here tomorrow

night, I'll see you get it."

"We ain't out on the streets," A-No. l answered. "Perfect order reigns. I never saw a more

law abidin' populace. There's no use callin' it names"

The Policeman held out his hand for the turkey.

"You just give me that."

"The sale was final."

The Policeman was desperate.

"You keep the turkey, I'm taking the kid."

A-No. l stared at the men, his expression one of utter confusion.

"What turkey? Turkey? Who sees a turkey?"

He looked the 'bos over. No one saw a turkey.

"What you see is a dog."

Barks and yaps and baying from the tramps as A-No. l looked them over for confirmation,

"What'd I tell you?"

Laughter, cackling, wheezing, along with the slapping of thighs and stomping, the

Halfy with only one leg to stamp with, some with only one arm.

"I'm only doing what I'm commanded to do," the Policeman pleaded. "If you gentlemen could only understand that—"

The turkey gobbled. Everything stopped. A-No. l stared dumb-founded. He looked at the

Policeman hard and accusingly. "Look what you've done."

"What have I done?"

"He *thinks* he's a turkey."

An ashen half-smile tried the corner of the Policeman's mouth. But it was more a contortion.

About him the hoboes stared accusingly. His voice when he spoke was a croak.

"He's not a turkey. That's clear. He's a dog."

"A what?"

"A dog."

"I know he's a dog. *He* doesn't know it."

The Policeman tried to control his shaking, he couldn't. His life, he knew, was suspended by

threads. He looked down at the turkey.

"Nice doggie."

"Nothing. He's very confused," A-No. l shook his head. "Bark for him."

"What?"

"Bark."

The Policeman looked at the turkey. His lower jaw drooped open and a sound akin to a moan came out.

"Louder."

The Policeman tried again, this time a weak bark.

A-No. l shook his head.

"There must be cotton in my ears."

The Policeman threw his head back, bayed mournfully, and started half out of his skin. The arm holding the turkey had encircled him. The great hairy red face exploded with noxious fumes.

"A drink for this great lover of dogs!"

The Policeman lifted his hand to protest, found it filled with a tin of alcohol squeezed from

the Sterno.

"I'm a man of temperance!"

"Nonsense," A-No. l countered. "With this you could nurse a baby."

He bolted down a tin for himself, exhaled loud and contented.
"How kind it is."

"I have asthma, you see," the Policeman pleaded.

"In this place? Never. People live so long we have to shoot them."

Desperate to be out of this, the Policeman threw back his head, the alcohol well on its way before he realized what he'd done. Though there was a flicker of warning as the 'bos leaned forward, anticipating. It was a warning too late. The rot gut, strong enough to bleach the rust off a rail, tore at his innards. His eyes bulged.

"You have never felt better than you do at this moment, confess it," A-No. l counseled.

Steam all but pouring from his ears, the Policeman grabbed his belly, plunged through howling, hooting tramps into the trees. Indignant, A-No. l shook his head.

"The Governor can steal in this state and an honest man can't," he said.

And they were on him. The Pokey Stiff, the Grease Tail, the Halfy, hailing him, grabbing his free hand as he moved, speeches tumbling out, exuberant.

"How'd you come in?"

"Private compartment on the Cheyenne Mail," he answered.

"They was bughouse thinkin' they could knock you off!"

A-No. l looked about.

"Who's got togs?"

"He's going to do it, boys!" the Pokey Stiff exulted. "He's going all the way!"

"Nothin' with tails," said A-No. l, still searching. "When I'm ridin' the rods no damn skirt's goin' catch on somethin' and adjourn matters."

"Show 'em their best ain't good enough!" the Grease Tail added.

"Oh, I'm feelin' fierce, boys!" chimed in the Halfy, rubbing the stump of his missing leg.

They'd reached the standing box car.

"How about a little doggie for dinner," the Pokey Stiff said, ogling the turkey.

"Look how contented he is to see us," the Grease Tail chimed in.

"Save me the gizzard," A-No. l said, handing the bird to the Pok-ey Stiff as he turned, boarded the box car.

Inside the empty, A-No. l came face to face with Cigaret, huddled in a corner, the pain of all he'd suffered clearly revealed. He had no reserve left, nothing to call upon. Pacing back and forth before the boy, A-No. l said nothing, and for the longest time it appeared he never would.

"You look a perfect bank, kid," A-No. l finally opened the meet-ing, still pacing. "Treasurer of the sty. What's your name? Stand back. Take off your hat."

Cigaret made no move, he wore no hat.

"You come in here as if you was a Bad Actor. You're not. You're a Casual. A Bad Actor wears a hat. The bums you been bummin' around with are Gay Cats. You haven't run with a first class hobo yet. Where you been sleepin'?"

"Straw stacks."

"Speak up!"

"Straw stacks, barns," Cigaret answered, trying to force a firmer voice that was still little more than a croak.

"None of your impudence. Who you think you're talkin' to? You slept out, say so. Have you got any money?"

"Couple of pennies."

"Are you willin' to be searched?"

Cigaret starts to reach for his money.

"You're a punk, a prushun. No tramp worth a damn's going to let himself be picked over. How long you been out, thirty days?"

Cigaret swallowed against the spasms deep in his bowels urging him to vomit.

"Bet you threw them western stiffs nearly wild, the way you tossed your feet. Given good weather and a lot of wide-eyed women, bet you cleared a nickel a day, pennies every time. Tried one of those Arapaho squaws? What'd you do, bawl like the devil, like you wanted to see your mama? If there's anything I can't take to it's homely baw-lin' kids. You can chew the rag with a stiff and he ain't goin' to cost you. A kid is somethin' else."

Cigaret looked down.

"Get your head up! What do you think you are, a bankrupt? What do you think you learned, how much?"

Cigaret slowly lifted his head.

"I'm gonna tell you somethin'," A-No. l still paced, a sudden moderation in his tone. "Get the cotton outa your ears and pay up. You got a chance to be a good bum, a meat eater, kid. From your looks it's plain if you had less brains you'd end up in a zoo. I'm not bein' kind to you. I could be your Uncle Mose and tell ya to join the Army. Soldiers is apes, kid, and you're too smart for that. You want to be a genuine blowed-in-the-glass stiff? I want to see you rough as a jungle buzzard, more'n somethin' just ready for a half-grown girl. Keep going the way you're goin', get sloughed up, kicked in all the weak places till the kicks don't hurt and run with the train. Remember that. But don't never grab on 'less you're certain. You ever let go she'll throw you under."

The Grease Tail ran into the opening, tossed a pile of clothing onto the threshold of the car, headed off for more. A-No. l picked up a shirt, ragged, torn. He weighed it a moment.

"How good a thief are you, kid?" he asked.

The Platte River, back eddies and swirls, coursed along the banks a quarter mile upstream from the yards. It was evening, late summer, and the river was shallow. A throng of locals, many dressed only in white baptismal gowns, women, men. children, crowded about a Preacher, three feet deep and twenty feet out from the bank. His hands pressed downward, into the water, immersing a sinner. His eyes were wild with salvation, his voice exhorting the Promised Land.

"Oh, Lord, give deliverance to this poor sinner!"

He pulled up the sinner, stripped to his long johns. He was A-No. l.

"I'm washed in the blood of the lamb!" cried the tramp.

"Trust in the Lord!" exhorted the Preacher.

"I feel his workings within me! I'm purified!" answered A-No. l.

Down he went again, the Preacher on top of him, the throng breaking into wild singing.

"You got to cross that River Jordan... you got to cross it for yourself... oh, there cain't nobody cross it for you... you got to cross it for yourself!"

"Tomorrow they'll give you the heavens," the Preacher sermonized over the chanting, "and then he'll give you the sea—"

He pulled up A-No. l.

"The Lord is my tabernacle!" A-No. l cried out, gasping for air.

"His ship is lined with gold!" the Preacher cried.

"Set sail for the pearly gate!" A-No. l answered.

Down he went again as the throng resumed its chant, swaying back and forth in the river.

"Cain't your brother cross it for you… you got to cross it for yourself… you got to stand the test of Judgement… you got to stand it for yourself—!"

On the bank, an Elder, naked to the waist, in his drawers, ran down to the river's edge, his face cardinal, yelled out, possessed. "Some son of a bitch stole our clothes!"

Under a trestle, the worshipers' clothes were in a pile, A-No. 1 and Cigaret picking over them quickly. Stripped to his waist, A-No. l revealed a hideous discoloration on his side, evidence that ribs had been broken, most likely from his earlier tumble from the train. Cigaret, who's found a belt, did not notice, so involved was he with the adventure.

"We'll take him when he comes off the turn," he chortled, puffed up like a rooster. "I'll come at him, look for an empty. If I see one I'll holler."

A-No. l looked at the boy with disdain, shook his head.

"What the hell have you learned, kid, I asked ya, more'n how to wipe snot from your beak?"

"See, here—"

"Anything?"

"Bet your life I has."

"Rattle it off, how much?"

"We can beat that son of a bitch!"

"Go on."

"There ain't a bull on this road who ain't gonna know my moniker."

"That it?"

"I got *this* far," Cigaret answered, flaring.

"I've changed my mind, kid," A-No. l answered.

"Huh?"

"Get back to that corn field with the punks."

"Wait a min, listen—"

"Whine at back doors, beg for scoffins." As Cigaret opened his mouth to protest, "You don't think that Shack knows damn well what empties he's got? Get yourself a tomato can, mooch for pennies—"

"I ain't a punk!"

"This ain't foolin', you listenin'?"

"Ask 'em in Toledo, ask St Loo—"

A-No. l started away.

"So long, kid."

"I'm listening," Cigaret caved.

"Twist that kerchief round your neck, tighten your belt, turn up your collar! You do what you're told you'll end up Emperor of the North, you do it right."

"Emperor's knows a lot" the boy said eagerly.

"Emperors knows a helluva lot. A-No. l knows more."

In the Kearney crew room, it was five-thirty the next morning, a time when the Yardmen were an hour into their work day. The Cracker was holding court. And a bottle. He poured into tins held by trainmen and crewmen, but his hand had a noticeable shake and his voice, a note higher it seemed, betrayed the after effects of a battle hard fought and not easily won. But won.

"He was bughouse thinking he could take on Shack. You ain't going to do that anymore'n stepping in the ring with Dempsey. You try to teach Shack that kind of lesson, you're going get reformed—"

When the door burst open. A Dinger, wild with excitement, showed his head inside.

"Jesus Christ! On the tower!"

In the Kearney yards a gondola glided down gravity tracks, the Shack riding out the bumper. The gondola collided with a box car, coupling, the Shack dropping in the tack pin, an Air Monkey securing the brake hose.

Up tracks a yard engine pulled a reefer ahead of a turnout. A Ground Hog bent a switch bar. The yard engine reversed, backed the reefer onto gravity tracks. Still pre-dawn a train was making up in the yards.

The Shack swung off the gondola, cut across tracks. A squalid row of houses stood at the edge of the yards. They were cribs. Red lights shone on the outside of several. They were lanterns, each belonging to a crewman and bearing the number of his train so that he could be identified and summoned when called for. Thus the red light district came by its name.

Reaching a lantern with a clearly marked '19', the Shack kicked open the door. A woman shrieked. A man bawled a startled oath. The Shack called in.

"Wrap it up Coaly. We're out of here in an hour."

The door left open, the Shack withdrew, started toward the terminal, stopped at the sight of the Cracker. He was running, sweat pouring down his face, drew to a stop ten yards away, almost in a crouch, lips parted in fear of one bearing malevolent news.

The Shack stared, realization quickly forming. A look of rage, terrible and fearful, forged upward from his bowels. He took a step toward the Cracker, then veered off sharply, broke into a run.

On the tower catwalk in the Kearney yards, the Shack came off the ladder, muscled his way through a throng of Yardmen gathered on the platform, stared speechless as others ran in from the yard, climbed the ladder. Pushing his way through the group, the Shack moved in beside his Hogger, stopped at the sight of scrawling written in charcoal on the face of the tower:

A-No. l B.E. Omaha 19. 10/25/31

The Shack pulled back, his anger ripe, rich, but in control as all on the tower looked to see his reaction. A slow grim smile pulled at his face.

THE SHACK STOOD WITH HIS LANTERN at the head of his engine, washed in the faint rays of a late summer sunrise. His face was violent. Behind him, the engine breathed deeply, and behind the engine was the new makeup of cars consisting of reefer, gondola, first of three box cars, stock car with a compliment of baying cattle, flat car loaded with lumber, second, then third box car, empty flat car and caboose. Ahead, the tracks ran eastward out of Kearney, through cottages, then into cornfields.

The Shack held, then turned, moved back toward the engine, past Yardmen huddled in small tense groups. There was no gaiety, no levity among them. Their mood was awe and forbidding. And something else. To a man, there wasn't one who didn't relish the thought of the Shack taken down. His contempt for each and every one of them, so freely expressed, was that resented. But they were working men in hard times with no affection for those who supped freely at the trough.

They, too, were there, the barnacles, the parasites, across the tracks, peering out from the edge of their jungle. Among them were runaways, thieves, the wanted and unwanted, society's relics, prideless, some with histories, others with none at all. But for a time, a short time, this time, then, they were accounted for. It was a battle of champions. They had never had their own before.

Reaching the engine, the Shack nodded down train to the Cracker, indicating the brakeman was to take up his post. In the cab the Coaly was feeding the fire box from the tender. The Hogger released air from the brakes as the Shack climbed aboard, looked down at his watch.

"6:40," he said.

The Hogger checked his time piece, verified the time.

"6:40."

The Shack held his gaze on the Hogger. The old engineer did not meet the Shack's eyes. He stared out his driver's side window, fixed on the track. His lips were very dry. His tongue ran over them. The Shack checked to verify the train's orders properly hung from the clip above the Hogger's chair, looked at the Coaly. Sweat poured off the Negro's body. The Shack reached overhead, gave the whistle two long blasts. At the initial turnout ahead, the Groundhog's lantern rose and fell, the signal to get going. The Hogger pushed the gear lever forward with his right hand. His left depressed the throttle bar.

The engine leaned her weight against the resistance of its trailing cars, snorted in protest as its wheels began to roll. In the engine's cab the Shack, glowing lantern still in hand, climbed up and stood on the gangway, stared over cars toward the rear of the train, soon saw what he was looking for. The caboose, following its trail of cars, was clearing the spur, its green port side light swinging into sight, followed by a white light from the Cracker telling the train had cleared its first turnout.

The Shack quit the gangway, dropped to the ground on the right side of the engine. He allowed the tender to go by, a car, two cars. Grabbing a handrail, he swung onto the bumpers at the end of the gondola. Darkening his lantern, he peered ahead.

Up track, Kearney switchmen bent switchbars, taking the train across a series of turnouts, its engine moving at a crawl, unable to generate speed as it headed through the yards leading out to the main.

On the roof of the caboose, the Cracker peered down, a programmed sentinel, as the train crawled past the water tower and stock yard. A warehouse slipped by, and the roundhouse. Everything was crimson in the first light of day.

Movement! The Shack saw it first, then the Cracker catching sight of a fleeting, darting figure moving in an out of train cars on an adjacent spur... .

Nothing. A dog.

The train, continuing its crawl through the yard, the Shack crossed to the opposite, right side of the gondola, then back to the left again, searching forward toward the engine, looking back toward the caboose, when passing the cribs, the sun in his eyes, it came, a great outrageous apparition bolting from between houses, clearing the distance between the cribs and the tracks in five immense strides. Leaping aboard the bumper between the gondola and the following box car, it disappeared from sight.

The Shack had seen the boarding, was off the left side of the gondola and running. The

Cracker, atop the caboose, had seen it too, was off the right side of the car. It was then, given his

anticipated moment, Cigaret drove in unseen from an adjacent track of sheltering empties down train from the Cracker as the Shack reached the stock car, pounded aboard, his lantern coming down to crown A-No. l. Except there *was* no A-No. l.

With an oath, the Shack was off the left side. Seeing nothing toward the rear of the train, he ran forward with the first box car, boarded, gaining the bumper at the same moment as the Cracker boarded from the right. Empty. Climbing fast up rungs to the roof of the car, the Shack peered out, saw nothing, looked forward toward the engine, then to the rear. Still nothing. Dropping back to the bumpers, the Shack and the Cracker regained the ground, each on opposite sides of the train.

Running forward with the slowly moving trail of cars, the Shack and Cracker, each on opposite sides of the train, moved slower than the train itself, examining empty blinds and platforms as cars moved past. Swinging onto the platform at the rear of the caboose, the Shack and the Cracker climbed to its roof, the Shack leaping forward onto the empty flat car, the Cracker holding position, watching both the sides of the train, able to detect any attempt to board as the Shack continued forward over roof tops, searching couplings and decks, holding to his jog, no matter the sway and heave beneath him, gained the end of the lumber atop the leading flat car, leaped to the roof of the forward box car filled with bawling longhorns.

Reaching the tender, the Shack had moved the length of the train, looked back, face creased with bewilderment, toward the rear the train, now cleared of the yard, accelerating, too fast for any man to board.

In the engine cab, the Coaly offered a congratulatory grin and cup of coffee as the Shack dropped down onto the gangway. Ignoring the coffee, the Shack looked reflectively back down train. His brain was in turmoil as he tried to assess what he'd missed. He turned to accept the coffee, stopped as it came to him. On the tender's backhead was a new coil of bell-cord tied to a coupling pin. Grabbing the cord, looping it over his shoulder, the six pound pin dangling down at his side, the Shack moved up and out of the cab onto the tender, headed down train.

Over roof tops, jumping from tender to reefer to gondola, the Shack grabbed the gondola's brake wheel, swung down the end ladder to the coupling between the gondola and the forward box car where he'd seen A-No. 1 board. Straddling the coupling, one foot on the bumper of the stock car, the other on the bumper of the gondola, the Shack lowered the coupling-pin down to the track, began to pay out the cord.

Underneath the stock car, Cigaret occupied the rods at the up train end of the trucks. He looked down, saw what was happening. The coupling pin, attached to the bell cord, played out by Shack as before, was striking the ties beneath the car, rebounding, a murderous, lethal missile. Cigaret pulled back, above the play of the pin. From his perch, he was clearly immune as more and more of the cord was played out, Cigaret following it, then looking the length of the undercarriage at A-No. 1 occupying the rods at the down train end of the car. The coupling pin, played back and forth, spit sparks off the rails as it worked its way down train, snaking toward A-No. 1.

No place to go, no escape, the older tramp looked toward Cigaret, the boy staring transfixed as A-No. 1 received the first cruel blow from the pin.

"Grab the cord!" A-No. 1 called out, shouting toward Cigaret. "*Grab it!*"

Cigaret threw out his hand to gab the cord—but didn't. His hand froze in midair, although all he had to do was wrap his fingers about it. He looked down train at A-No. 1.

A-No. 1 saw what was happening, even as the pin struck him again, cracking his cheekbone, an audible pop. The hideous churning and rattling of trucks and coupling pin like a chorus of anvils, A-No. 1 stared imploringly at the boy. Cigaret held his hand still poised out over the cord, then withdrew it completely, unwilling to offer assistance.

A-No. 1 had no moment to reflect as the coupling pin struck his body again, showering flecks of blood. He had only one choice, one salvation. As Cigaret watched with morbid fascination, A-No. 1 eased himself out of the truck, down onto the gunnel, directly into the path of the flying coupling pin. What he was after the boy quickly learned. A-No. 1's foot inched out till it struck a thin rod. There was a sharp prolonged hissing. With all the force at his command, A-No. 1 rammed his foot against it. It was the air brake rod.

With a terrible screech of metal on metal, the Shack was thrown against the down train end of the box car. His head, striking hard, stunning him, he fought to keep from going under the wheels.

In the engine cab, the Coaly was nearly pitched through the engine's fire door into the firebox, the Hogger grabbing the gear bar, hauling it into neutral.

The Shack, off the woods between the box car and stock car, had stumbled to the ground. Blood poured from a gash on the side of his head. Like a great gored bull, he made a futile lunge after Cigaret as he came out from under the stock car. Turning, the Shack stumbled down train as it lurched to a stop.

In the engine cab, the Coaly writhed on the floor. His back had been seared, the pain all but blinding him. The Hogger dropped beside him, breathing heavily, hand on his own chest from broken ribs, blinking his eyes in a stupid sort of way as he tried to figure what to do.

The Shack, the right side of his face awash in blood, ran toward the rear of the train, slammed aboard the caboose, entered it, words flying from his mouth.

"*Damn* you, Cracker son of a bitch! I tell you something, by Jesus, you do it—!"

His voice trailed off as he saw the Cracker sprawled face down on the steps leading up to the cupola. Blood poured from his head, eyes open, sightless.

Cigaret thrashed through weeds, moving up track, ahead of the stalled train. Directly above him was the road bed, below him a thirty foot slope to a river. He was exhilarated, worked to a frenzy, a wolf cub who had just tasted his own first kill. But he knew A-No. l's fury, knew it would come as a charge, a maddened primitive drive out of the weeds. He was sure of that, kept to the upper reaches of the embankment, ready to bolt, up or down.

Suddenly, his feet flew out from under him. Not from any physical act, but from what he all at once saw. He backpedaled furiously, nearly to the top of the incline, held there, wide-eyed as he looked down. At the base of the embankment, A-No. l squatted at the edge of the river, thirty, forty feet below. He was hurt. He would not admit it, would not show pain. He was down on his haunches, washing his wounds, prominent and considerable.

"What's the matter?" Cigaret came on hard. "You look broke up to me."

Cigaret's heels dug into the dirt, ready to push himself up and away as A-No. l's great head came slowly around. He regarded the boy as if by watching he might discern the key to some mystery that hitherto had escaped him.

"I can fight like a house afire if that's what you want," the boy blustered on. "I'm ready."

A-No. l held, turned back to the river and his wounds.

The action unnerved Cigaret, and excited him. "You're broke up bad, you're quitting," he said.

No answer.

"Drag your ass back to the Jesus shouters," Cigaret swaggered on, "and tell 'em they got a Stew Bum for the choir. This 'bo's headn' out, he's on the way. And that ain't just to look around. He's goin' to parade, high monkey-monk of everything, tramp royal. Emperor of the North! Slashin' right and left with my razor, puttin' my fist into more faces'n you can figger."

He kicked at the loose soil, started a small landslide, cascading down, waited for the answer that didn't come.

"I'm talkin' straight, you better listen. I ain't stickin' with you anymore."

Below, by the river, A-No. l had not stopped washing his wounds. But his eyes told it. Masking a soul of a thousand guises, they masked none now. His face was leaden, filled with foreboding.

Cigaret pulled back and away. "You ain't good for bummin' no more," the boy crowed in conclusion. "You ain't mean enough for it."

In the engine cab, the shack furiously shoveled coal into the fire box. It was heavily fueled. Flames licked through the opening. On the floor of the cab, the Coaly was immobilized with pain and worse. The Hogger's face was twisted with emotion as he tried to remove the remains of the Coaly's shirt, tried to apply grease.

Slamming down the shovel, the Shack checked water and steam gauges, cut off the air brakes. "Take her out," he ordered the Hogger.

The old engineer didn't move. He couldn't. He shook with fear.

The Shack grabbed him by the collar. "I'll put this engine out of business," he warned. "You know what that'll be for you? You go when she goes!"

Still, the Hogger froze.

Seizing the gear lever, the Shack pushed it forward, depressed the throttle bar. The engine worried its aching body into motion, then lunged forward. Reaching down, the Shack grabbed the Hogger by the collar, lifted him onto his feet, planted him before his controls. "When I hit the rooftops, high ball!"

Grasping his hammer, the Shack quit the cab, went up over the top of the train, looked left side, right, moved on down over roof tops.

In the engine cab the Hogger did as told, shoved the throttle to the max. The engine's wheels spun, a shower of sparks, then caught, slowly, reluctantly began to answer the command.

A-No. l had climbed from the river, was set to sprint from the weeds, all at once stared as he saw Cigaret bolt from the embankment, boarding the up train end of the stock car, and was climbing to its roof. Two cars up train, the Shack was on the gondola, moving down train, searching couplings and blinds, saw Cigaret at the same moment Cigaret saw the Shack.

Cigaret panicked. Pushing off the edge of the down train edge of the stock car he leaped to the flat car loaded with lumber, came down on his ankle, twisting it painfully. No time to nurse injuries, he crawled along the lumber against the increasing buck and heave of the train as the Shack moved down the roof off the forward box car, leaped to the stock car in pursuit. His movements, unlike Cigaret's, were unhurried. Time was not a factor. Distance was. And he narrowed it over roof tops with experienced caution watching Cigaret heading headlong into failure.

Reaching the end of the third and final box car, Cigaret came off it onto the second of the train's two flat cars, an empty, limped toward the final car, the caboose.

The Shack's voice mocked his effort. "Oh, you can run, kid. But you're running out of train!"

Crossing the flat car, Cigaret reached the caboose, grabbed the up train ladder, scrambled up, came off it onto the roof, spilling him as he reached it. He did not go over, but the Shack was gaining. Painfully scrambling to his feet, Cigaret plunged headlong toward the end of the car, reached it, his hand lowering to the grab iron atop the end ladder. But there was no grab iron. Nor end ladder either. Nor side ladder, left or right. All had been removed. With a sickening look of fear, Cigaret stared back at the empty flat car, pitching, swerving, an eight-foot drop. Such acrobatics were beyond him, not with that ankle.

Planting his feet on the roof, Cigaret hunched forward, red hot cinders playing back from the engine stack like tracer bullets as the Shack emerged off the up train ladder, hammer in hand. Cigaret was backed to the edge of the roof. There was no place to go. His breath was a wheeze as fifty feet separated the pair. The roof rocked and swayed.

The Shack pounded the hammer into his fist. "You got it coming, kid. You're overdue, no doubt about it." A sudden lurch of the train and the Shack dropped to one knee to maintain his balance. His rage was white-hot as he savored the moment of showdown. "My brakey's cracked his neck. Hide's peelin' off the black and Hogger's coutin' his broke ribs." He rose and started toward Cigaret, smoke swirling past him. "All because of you, kid." The agony of indecision. To jump from the speeding train was suicidal. Yet the Shack was moving closer, within fifteen feet.

Cigaret backed to the farthest edge of the caboose, his injured leg all but crumbling, when:

"Your fight's over here, Shack!"

The Shack spun about. A-No. 1 stood on the up train edge of the caboose's roof. Staring through blood smeared teeth, a look of utter stupefaction on his face, the Shack held on A-No. 1, thirty feet away, then moved, cocked and let go with his hammer. A-No. 1 was already coming on hard. The hammer hit him, a glancing blow on the right side of his leg, the Shack following, driving his shoulder into A-No. 1's mid-section, plowing him backward, the two men sailing off the roof top, the Shack in A-No. 1's grasp. The bed of the empty flat car took the fall of both with an audible crunch.

The impact of the fall broke A-No. 1's hold on the Shack, sent him bounding to the edge of the fat car. The Shack, separated from A-No. 1, rolled over, clutching his kneecap shattered in the fall. But the power of his will and hatred for the tramp was more than a match for the injury. Coming to his feet, he limped, half hopped, half ran, stiff legged to the end of the down train end of the flat car, crossed onto the platform at the end of the caboose. Hanging from pegs was a veritable arsenal of hammers, lanterns, knuckle pins, chains.

At the far end of the flat car, A-No. 1 lifted his head, blinked at the sight of the Shack reboarding the flat car. Moving with a locked right leg, in the Shack's right hand was a hammer. In his left a three foot length of chain, doubled back on itself, wrapped around the Shack's wrist.

On the roof of the caboose, Cigaret had come to its up train end, wanting to continue on, away, up train, but held there, no way to pass the Shack below. He looked toward A-No. 1, saw him struggling to his feet, saw the Shack approaching, his weapons held out on front of him, the trainman's face, positively primitive, ferocious.

A-No. 1 looked at the Shack, and he looked past him, at the arsenal at the end of the caboose. The Shack caught the look. A terrible, muscular half-grin pulled at his mouth as he came on, stalking. A-No. 1 moved left and right from side to side of the flat car, then drove, trying to get past. The Shack had anticipated the move, swung with the chain, caught A-No. 1 as he passed. The links cracked against

A-No. 1's back whipping him back onto the deck. With more agility than his shattered leg should permit, the Shack restationed himself between the tramp and the caboose.

A-No. 1 lifted himself onto all fours. The Shack's hammer flailed down, knocked A-No. 1's arm out from under him. Raising the chain overhead, the Shack brought it down, A-No. 1 barely able to roll free as the chain struck the bed of the flat car gouging out wood. Backing away, the Shack watched as A-No. 1 struggled painfully back to his feet, blinked through pain and realization. The Shack had slow death in mind.

On the roof of the caboose above, Cigaret had dropped to his belly, was peering over the edge in shock as the Shack came on again, flailing out with the chain, A-No. 1 recoiling, but not quite enough, the tip of the chain catching him on the side of the face, again sending him to the boards. Still the Shack would not move in for the kill. He waited, hovering, wanting A-No. 1 with his full senses to taste, to watch and feel what was happening.

Suddenly, unexpectedly, A-No. 1 bolted. With a force derived from all his inner resources, he tried to move past Shack. The chain came down again, across his back, sprawling him, the Shack between A-No. 1 and the caboose. No hurry. All in command.

From the roof of the caboose, Cigaret watched in gathering fear. For himself. The death of the super tramp would leave him next and he knew it. The clanging of chains and irons against the wall of the caboose below him reached his ears. He eased himself out over the edge looked down. They were out of his reach, but even if they were, what did he think he could do with them? He looked toward A-No. 1.

The tramp rolled over onto his back, staring up at the heavy sweating face above him. He broke into a contemptuous sneer. "Bastard!"

Bile welled up in the Shack's throat. Bile and hatred. He lifted the chain, a deliberate move, too much so. A-No. 1's arm shot up, grabbed the chain coming down. With all the force at his command he pulled down hard. The chain, wrapped around the Shack's wrist, yanked the Shack off his feet, across A-No. 1, to and over the edge of the flat car.

As Cigaret stared bug-eyed, A-No. 1, in a crouch, looked down at the Shack, dangling over the side of the car, feet bounding off the racing ties. All A-No. 1 had to do was release that chain to send the Shack to a crushing end. The Shack gave him no reason to do otherwise. There was no pleading, no begging. Trapped as he was, he flailed out with his hammer in his free hand, trying for all he was able to take the tramp with him.

Watching in disbelief, no way to understand, Cigaret saw A-No. 1 grab the Shack, lift him back onto the flat car, yank the chain free from the Shack's grasp, stand, legs spread, between the caboose and the Shack, waiting for the Shack to rise. The Shack measured A-No. 1. He measured the chain. And he weighed the hammer still in his own hand. He flailed out with it, took a blow on the side of his head, flailed out again, took another blow from the chain, dropped to the floor of the car. A-No. 1 stood back from him, waited for him to regain his feet, the roles now reversed. Twice more, the Shack tried to connect with his hammer, twice more the chain cracked into him. On his knees, bleeding from mouth and eyes, the Shack held, head down.

Ten feet away, A-No. 1 waited, knowing the man had one last move. It came. With all the strength he had left, the Shack threw his hammer. A-No. 1 had seen the move, tried to avoid it, the hammer striking him, sending him toppling, writhing, to the deck of the car. The Shack drove in, great arms outstretched, hands spread like two huge claws closing to clamp on A-No. 1's throat.

It never happened. A-No. 1 exploded from his crouch, caught the Shack mid-section with his shoulder. The force of the Shack's charge, and the up thrust of A-No. 1's drive, sent the Shack up over A-No. 1. He landed on his back, slid along the deck, like an upturned beetle, desperately struggled for handholds. But there were no handholds. There was nothing. Only air as he went over, cartwheeled off the side of the flat car, down onto the embankment, bounced along with the train, then disappeared into the weeds.

A-No. 1 was down on all fours, staring after his conquered foe as Cigaret, staring too, came off the caboose's up train ladder, leaped across to the flat car, turned to A-No. 1, the thrill of victory in the boy's eyes, along with monumental relief and surging power. Ahead, the train was approaching a trestle that bridged swampy marshland. Testing his leg, testing his ribs, A-No. 1 saw the boy approaching, grinning, eyes agleam.

"Me and you," Cigaret chortled. "If we ain't the team. We'll go to prison and free the prisoners. We'll capture Mexico. Do in Rome as the Dagoes do, knock down everything we see, all stuck on ourselves. Cigaret and A-No. 1."

He reached A-No. 1, beamed up at the tramp. A look came into A-No. 1's face. A gentle look, filled with warmth and understanding. There was a hollow roar as the train headed onto the trestle.

"Kid—" Reaching out, A-No. 1 put his hands on Cigaret's shoulders. "You got no class."

The hands bit into the shoulders, lifted the boy off his feet, hurled him, literally, out over the side of the train, Cigaret falling, down over the trestle, into the marshy slew where he came up stunned and sputtering. On the flat car, A-No. 1 shouted after him, "Try the barns, kid! Run like the devil, find an empty! Get a can and take up moochin'! Tackle back doors for a nickel! Tell your story, make their eyes run! Only stay off the rails, give it up! It's a bum world for a bum! You'll never make Emperor of the North, kid! So long!"

Slashing the water in a futile pout, Cigaret stared after A-No. 1 and the train, speeding away.

THE END

You've read the book, now check out the movie— now on Blu-Ray disc...

... starring Lee Marin, Ernest Borgnine and Keith Carradine

www.ingramcontent.com/pod-product-compliance
Lightning Source LLC
Chambersburg PA
CBHW051146020726
47501CB00005B/1698